Theo Cross

Theo Cross

A Life Lived under Grace

Albert J. D. Walsh

WIPF & STOCK · Eugene, Oregon

THEO CROSS
A Life Lived under Grace

Wipf & Stock
An Imprint of Wipf and Stock Publishers
199 W. 8th Ave., Suite 3
Eugene, OR 97401

www.wipfandstock.com

ISBN 13: 978-1-62564-491-6

Manufactured in the U.S.A.

For Jessica

Contents

Foreword

As Pastor Theo Cross observes the cracks in the ceiling above his hospital bed, he sees in them the pattern of his life—lines crossing this way and that, broken in places, jutting out in all directions—a tapestry of people and events.

Chapter by chapter, Albert Walsh weaves the story of Theo Cross, a man of God, a man of faith, yet also a man facing his own weakness and brokenness. With vivid detail and raw emotion, Walsh deftly recounts, in a series of dream-dramas, the past events that brought Theo Cross to a life lived for his Lord, answering the "call" heard early in his life. In Theo's hospital room, past and present meet in the people whose lives Theo touches and who in turn touch his. Facing pain, uncertainty, fear, and death, Theo is seeking the God he has "thought" about all of his life.

As life slips away, Theo finds his God in the simple faith of Mr. Wagner; in the compassion of Father Jim O'Connor; in the questions of Mark Johnson – professor of philosophy; in the friendship and camaraderie of Rabbi Allen; and in the love and devotion of his wife, Doris, and daughter, Jessica. Each brings a measure of God's grace to Theo, as he, in return, brings a full measure to each of them.

The story of Theo Cross is a "good" story. It is the story of love, hope, and faith—a life lived under grace. As is the expressed hope of the author in the Preface, I can attest to the power of *Theo Cross*. "I laughed; I cried; it became a part of me!"

Preface

Between sacred and mundane stories there is a distinction without separation. From the sublime to the ridiculous, all people's mundane stories are implicit in its sacred story, and every mundane story takes soundings in the sacred story.

STEPHEN CRITES

ONCE LIBERATED FROM THE mind, imagination, and pen of the author, stories so often take on a life of their own. A good story touches us in the deepest regions of heart and soul, disclosing something real, something true and powerful. Stories enfold life and bring to light the emotions, experiences, and dynamics of human interaction that resonate with our very own personal histories. The names, faces, and character traits of those who populate the narrative are strangely familiar to the reader; it sometimes seems as though the author as storyteller has read and borrowed from the pages of human existence and encounter, contributing aspects of his or her own life story as well.

The characters in the narrative you are poised to enter are real to life, though they are not *real* people. The characters in this story have lived at some point in time, under a variety of names, and in a variety of places. One might even say that they are presently living, somewhere, today and will again tomorrow. Yet any relationship between characters in this story and "real" people is pure coincidence. What is not coincidental is the relationship between the characters in this story and other persons who, even at this moment, are living out each and every page within the diversities of being human.

In one of the first segments of that wonderful comedic sitcom titled *Night Court*, the two guards are standing side-by-side listening to a defendant plead his case before Judge Harry Stone. The tall, lanky fellow bends in the direction of his small female counterpart, whispering, "Selma, wasn't that a beautiful story?" And while staring straight ahead, in her typical dry wit, Selma responds, "I laughed; I cried; it became part of me!"

When a story works the mystery of its several intended purposes, when it discloses life and living with a clarity that is captivating, resonating with the life we know to be true, we too will laugh, cry, and maybe its truth will also then become part of who we are or hope to be. If a narrative is true to life, and the very best narratives are those capturing human life as manifest in its immense variety, and if our own identity takes shape as something like a narrative, then the stories we read—whether fiction or nonfiction—can readily become elements of our own identity narrative.

As the author and storyteller it is my profound hope that the reader will bear witness to the power of *Theo Cross: A life lived under Grace* by saying upon finishing, "I laughed; I cried; it became part of me!"

Acknowledgments

I WISH TO EXPRESS my gratitude to all who read this manuscript in its roughest form, and offered critical and extremely constructive insights, all of which immeasurably improved my writing style. I am only too aware of the debt owed them for the time and investment made in graciously improving this work in progress, making the story of *Theo Cross* a far more pleasurable read.

I am equally grateful to all those persons who played a huge part in sharing their stories with me, over the course of my pastoral ministry; while they remain nameless for reasons of confidentiality, I would hope that they will hear resonance of their own spiritual struggles and strengths in the characters of this short novel.

Finally, I am extremely grateful to each and all of those pastoral colleagues, who give so very much of heart, spirit, and self to the people they have been called to serve, and do so with grace, generosity of spirit, and great integrity; hopefully, they too will see in *Theo Cross* a familiar face, a colleague in pastoral ministry, and a companion in this "life lived under grace."

1

A Seasonal God

The world is never what it ought to be. Where there are men there is always failure, and where there is failure, the need is for improvement. What is deformed must be reformed. Hence, in the secular sphere, reform, and the constant introduction of new reforms, are simply taken for granted, not only by the crusading fanatic but equally by the man in the street, who spontaneously raises his voice in opposition to any bad state of affairs and demands that it be put right.

HANS KÜNG

THEO OPENED HIS EYES. For the longest time he lay staring at the ceiling tiles above his bed; select water stains and the occasional cracks running in each and every direction disclosed the age of the hospital building in need of repair. And then the thought came to him; the random pattern of the cracks reflected something of what he thought his life had been, at least the life he had lived thus far. He thought of his life as random and broken, or at least random-brokenness, with select stains-of-sin still evident, though only to the inner eye of conscience.

With only slight discomfort, more from the position he'd been in all morning than from any symptom of his ailment, Theo turned his head to the right. The large window provided a panoramic view of the city he loved and the sky above, gray and heavy with winter clouds. Gray, like the suit worn by his doctor on the day he'd been admitted to the hospital. Small flakes of snow began to fall; those touching the warmth of the windowpane would simply melt away. Theo thought about melting away, about becoming invisible, about *death*. The window would not hold his attention; then again, nothing human or common to "the order of creation" could hold the attention of Theo Cross for more than a moment of reflection.

In an almost unconscious twist of his head to the left, he turned to gaze down at his wrist. The long fingers of another hand seemed attached to his lower arm. Slowly he lifted his eyes from the sleeve to the elbow to the shoulder; white on white on white. The woman at his bedside was tall and thin with pale blue eyes, the dark circles beneath them bearing testimony to sleepless nights, or worse. She issued a set of numbers as though at a bingo game, "140 over 70, Mr. Cross. Not bad at all. Why don't you get some sleep?" Those long fingers pulled aside the pink curtain surrounding his bed, and she was gone as quickly as she had come into his room.

Theo returned his gaze to the cracks in the ceiling above, trying now to recall the thought they had engendered just moments ago. He knew it was about this life, something about *his* life. But what was the thought? It didn't matter at all, because now a new thought had come to mind "Brokenness, like human life before a holy and righteous God!" Was it a sermon title, or maybe the line from a book, perhaps part of a poem? The randomness of those cracks, the pattern of the tiles interrupted by lines running from left to right; the pattern of life broken by trials and hardships symbolized "Brokenness, like human life before God." Theo had often thought his life conformed to that classic line from Shakespeare's *Hamlet*: "When sorrows come, they come not in single spies, but in battalions!"

From the earliest days of his time spent in seminary Theo Cross distinguished himself as the one who always associated sorrows and suffering with the reality of God. When he couldn't think about anything else he could always think about God! God was the one topic that *could* hold the attention of Theo Cross for more than a moment. He could quite literally spend hours contemplating the reality of God's being; whether God was subject or object, or some combination of the two; God the absolute; God the loving and benevolent Father; God the judge of all—"God in three persons, blessed Trinity." In fact he'd once been told, "A person can have no higher calling or purpose in life than to think about God—thought being the first act of worship." For the moment Theo couldn't remember who had said that, but he was certain he'd heard it from someone who would know it to be true.

The snow now fell in a steady pattern of light and then heavy flakes. Theo thought about children, school, sleds, hills, and snowmen. He imagined some children, somewhere outside the city limits, throwing snowballs at each other with all the vengeance of warriors locked in mortal combat. Mortal combat. That's what we humans are all about, thought Theo, locked in a kind of mortal combat between the forces of good and those of evil. A voice somewhere within his soul whispered, "And who will win the day is anyone's guess!" Glibly, Theo accepted the comment; but then he remembered *God*.

"No," he whispered beneath his breath, "No! God will most surely win the Day!"

Once again Theo closed his eyes in the effort to follow the advice of his nurse and get some sleep. The night before had been sleepless with both physical and emotional pain violently pounding him from within. But sleep had never come easy to him, even in those days of his youth when he was vibrant and healthy. Now sleep was the pearl of great value that seemed always to be just beyond his reach, and well beyond the prayerful petitions of those who cared for him. The doctors warned that the pain would be severe and unrelenting, but Theo had no idea that pain could also be so terribly merciless in its pursuit of some pointless objective. The pain associated with cancer had always been someone else's, and that somehow made it easier for Theo to bear.

Prayer did help. Whenever a dull book of theology, or some dry reading of one of several manuals on ministry, did not bring-on the pleasure of much needed sleep, prayer helped. For Theo Cross, prayer "worked." He'd grown tired of staring at the cracks in the ceiling, trying to recall the exact meaning they held for life. He closed his eyes and thought; that's also how his prayers began, in thought. Sometimes his prayers ended that way as well; in thought. "The freedom of thought given wings in prayer" is how he'd once put in a sermon; "The freedom of thought given wings." Wings, for sure, but for what purpose? The wings of freedom, ascend above the fray, or fly away? Fight or flight!

Freedom. Theo thought about freedom and death. Was death a kind of freedom, and if it was—*from* what—and *for* what? Certainly death could mean freedom from pain, but the cost of that freedom seemed too high a price to pay. Freedom and death; the two words tasted like dry ash in his mouth and frightened him. Why in the name of God was he even thinking about death? He was supposed to be praying, wasn't he? The freedom of thought given wings . . . .

"*Never changing God, eternal Ruler of the universe, and gracious heavenly Father, help me in my hour of greatest need. Help me to sleep and find rest for my soul. You are always the same; your love never changes; you are day-to-day the same, generation to generation you are God. Bless all who suffer with your unfailing comfort. Amen.*" The prayer didn't bring sleep, so Theo opened his eyes and returned to what he knew best—thinking.

A shuffle of feet alerted him to the fact that a visitor had entered the room. First the shuffle of feet, and then the voice, barely audible, "Mr. Wagner, do you wish the sacrament?"

"Yes, father," was the reply of his roommate, "I'd like that very much. I missed you last week, so I'm glad you're here now."

Again there came the soft voice of the priest, "Yes, I'm here now."

The voices continued their sharing in hushed tones. For the first time since he'd been admitted to the hospital, Theo thought of the curtain between his bed and that of his roommate as a great pink wall, excluding him from some extraordinary event. He lay there, as still as death, hoping to hear something more, when suddenly that pink wall parted. The priest turned on his heels and headed for the door.

After the priest had left Theo thought, "Why haven't we yet reached the point of love's demand to share in that most blessed Sacrament?" It was then that he heard other feet just outside the door to the room and watched in silence as a woman in clerical dress entered and stood at his bedside, introducing herself to Theo as "Chaplain Grace." It was another of those realities Theo hadn't yet gotten used to, seeing a female in clerics. But this was Theo Cross, and his very next thought was a portion of scripture: "Neither Jew nor Greek, neither slave nor free, neither male nor female."

5

All are one in Christ. Chaplain Grace shared the Sacrament with Theo, offered a brief prayer, and left the room with a parting assurance, "I will pray for you." With that, Theo closed his eyes—and slept.

The prick of the needle awakened Theo from sleep. "Sorry Mr. Cross," said the technician "didn't intend to wake you."

"No problem," said Theo in a voice sounding like sandpaper on crystal, "I wasn't sleeping anyway; just resting my eyes, that's all."

The technician continued, "Your doctor thought it best we get some blood work done before your next treatment begins, just to see if there've been any changes, I mean *significant* changes in the blood count."

The large rubber band pinched his skin causing Theo to arch his brow. "How much of that stuff do you guys think I have in there? You keep drawing out at this rate and we needn't worry about the cancer killing me!"

The young technician, with a half-smile, said, "Well, we'll see that we don't take enough to . . . ," but chose not to complete the thought or the sentence.

Seeing what he thought to be distress or embarrassment on the technician's face Theo said, "That's alright young man, I *know* I'm dying."

Without another word the lab tech picked up all of the waste paper from the edge of the bed, threw the vile of blood collected in his carryall, and headed for the door. Theo thought how strange it must be to have a job in which one spent the entire day dealing with human blood.

The nurse came into the room in her usual punctual fashion, "So, how are my two favorite patients doing?"

Both Theo and Wagner replied, in a similar fashion and with the same falsehood, "Just fine!"

She approached each patient's bed and took it upon herself to elevate the head of each. "Dinner's on the way," she said as she exited the room, "I want you *both* to eat *everything* on your platters, you hear?"

When the nurses would talk in that way, Theo always cringed, feeling it was demeaning and implied that he was a child, incapable of making his own choices responsibly, even though he supposed the nurses also had the best of intentions for the patients.

"I mean it now," she continued, "I'll have none of this half-eaten dinner stuff!"

Theo didn't say a word; it was Wagner who spoke, "Okay, Okay! For Christ's sake, just bring in the food!"

Nurse Howard made the final adjustments on both portable bedside stands, moving the trays to the appropriate level, and then went to retrieve the dinner platters. Only seconds later she entered the room again, placing first Wagner's and then Theo's tray on the respective stands. Stepping back and taking her position between her "two favorite patients," she reminded them, "Now remember, every bit of it *gone* by the time I return from dinner myself."

Theo and Wagner nodded—like obedient children.

Theo lifted the lid on his tray; a breast of broiled chicken, some mashed potatoes, green beans, salad, ice cream and Sanka. The meals were always adequate, but both patients could always find some reason to complain. For a long time they both sat, staring at their trays. As if on command they both bowed their heads, offering a prayer of thanksgiving for the food they wouldn't eat—despite the nurse's command. Theo was deep in thought; he was thinking about meal-time in another place, another time, with others.

Mealtime in the Cross household had always been a time for family conversation. Theo thought about the several discussions they had over a period of about two weeks in which each member of the family offered his or her opinion on the existence of God. He thought about how much he'd looked forward to mealtime and their conversations, even though it didn't appear that others at table shared his enthusiasm for the topic of choice—*his* choice. Theo took a quick glance over at his roommate who was taking his fork to that breast of chicken, pulling first the flesh from the meat and then the meat from the bone with deliberate force.

He really didn't know all that much about his roommate, about Wagner, his "condition" or his "prognosis." Only three days before he'd overheard a conversation between Wagner and one of his family members which suggested that his "condition" wasn't very good or the "prognosis" all that promising. Theo thought about the scene which had transpired earlier, with the priest. Without looking over at Wagner, Theo asked his roommate, "Have you been a Catholic all your life?" Only silence.

Leaning over his bed rail Theo rephrased his question, "How long have you been a Catholic?" "All my life, I suppose. At least that's all I've ever known. Before me, my parents, grandparents, great-grandparents. I don't know just how far back, but we've always been Catholic. My whole family belongs to the Church; we go to Mass every Saturday; never miss. Why'd you ask?"

"Just curious," said Theo with some reluctance to pursue this any further, thinking maybe he'd opened a can of worms. Still, this was the Rev. Theo Cross, so he couldn't resist and pressed on, "Do you think about God?"

"Think about God?" The question seemed strange to Wagner, but as he thrust his fork into another piece of broiled chicken, holding it to his mouth, he said, "I don't think much about God; I never miss Mass."

"You mean to say you don't think about God *at all*?" Theo wasn't noticing the expression on the face of his roommate as he continued, "I mean, you *never* think about God, or what God is like?"

Wagner swallowed the piece of chicken breast, took a deep breath, turned his eyes on Theo and said, "God? I guess I think about God from time to time. Most the time, I just believe. What is it you want to know?"

Supposing his question could have been misconstrued and offensive, even though he never intended to offend or intrude, Theo justified his questioning by assuring himself that he was only trying to make conversation. For the moment he thought it best to change the subject, talk about something less threatening, a topic *other than* God. "Why are you in?" he asked. "What's the problem?"

"I'm dying," was the response, blunt, almost without hesitation. "Just like you, *Pastor* Cross, I'm dying, Cancer of the liver."

Theo wondered how Wagner had learned that he was ordained. Maybe he lived somewhere near the church Theo served? Perhaps he'd seen his picture in the paper? All of that no longer held his attention; another, more urgent, question pressed Theo to ask, "And how do you feel about dying?"

Leaning forward in his bed, Wagner whispered, "What is this anyway, some kind of pastoral counseling session?" He wasn't smiling; his glare was discomforting; he wanted an answer, but the answer would never come.

Digging his fork into the white meat of the chicken breast for the last piece, and with a force sufficient to crack the bone, Wagner continued, "You clergy-types—are all alike! You think people have to open their heart and soul to you. You think it makes things better when a person talks about the pain—death." There was a long pause and then, "Come on pastor, what difference *how* I feel about it? I'm dying! What'd you want me to say?"

Years of pastoral care had never prepared Theo for such occasions; even the excessive reading and study he'd done on his own and over the years of ministry had never adequately prepared him for such moments as this. Still, he was familiar with the moments when one question opened the flood gates of another person's soul, moments when honesty came disguised in the garb of genuine despair; moments when the candor of emotion caught him off-guard.

Theo felt what he'd always felt in such circumstances; he felt out-of-control, yet somehow deeply and deliberately concerned. Yes, he knew that he was into something he couldn't evade, and yet felt no need, no urgency, to shake off the "seriousness" of the moment. Turning to his own platter he ate selectively from the potatoes and green beans. Theo never cared much for chicken, perhaps because his parishioners had always called it "pastor food," a remainder from those days when, in some settings of the church in rural and poorer parishes, pastors actually received their compensation in the form of chickens and other food from farmers, having nothing more to share as compensation. The Sanka was tolerable. Timidly, yet thoughtfully, Theo asked, "Doesn't the fact that you're dying make you think even *more* about God?"

Wagner turned to gaze at Theo. "Why should death make me think even *more* about God? It's a fact of life. People die every day of the week. Are they all thinking even *more* about God? I'm not even sure I see the tie between death and God. What're you driving at?"

Taking another gulp of Sanka, Theo gathered all his theological faculties together and then continued, "Well it seems to me that there's an important relationship between death and God. For instance, how can a God of goodness, mercy, and love permit such suffering and despair as you and I are experiencing? Death brings dread, anxiety,

sadness, and more questions than answers. Isn't an all powerful God somehow accountable for this?"

Wagner said, "You make this conversation sound like
a seminary course, or like an examination for the priesthood! I don't know about some all-powerful God; I'm not
even sure that God cares about our little individual prob-
lems or 'sufferings' as you said. It's just a fact of life, Pastor
Cross, so why not just consent to it?" Wagner pushed his
tray to the side, "Why look for answers to questions nobody
else seems concerned with? I think you clergy treat life as
though it were some form of cosmic classroom, with God
standing at the head of the class, chalk in hand, just waiting to answer questions." Staring into his empty coffee mug
Wagner concluded, "This is ridiculous; it's pointless; I don't
get why it's so important to you what I think about God,
death, or anything else for that matter!"

Theo now felt a greater concern for his roommate; he
could've sworn he *felt* Wagner's apprehension and anxiety
filling the space between them, it seemed palpable. "Look,"
he said softly, "I just thought that maybe you had some
questions of your own. I find that not a day goes by that I
don't have some question that touches on my faith, my belief, or my trust in a 'good and gracious' God. I don't think
the conversation 'pointless' at all; misguided, perhaps, but
not pointless."

Wagner hoisted himself up on his elbows, "I'm sorry
Pastor," he said, "I'm just anxious, tense. I didn't mean to
snap at you like that. It's just that I'm in no mood to be
answering questions about the meaning of life, death, and
God when the meaning of my own life now hangs in the
balance and death is coming any day now. I'm sorry."

There was a moment of silence, a long and uncom-
fortable moment. Wagner bowed his head, almost as if in
prayer, and said, "Sometimes I think about God. Maybe

that's why I love living in this part of the country, I mean with the change of seasons. I enjoy the changes coming and the surprises they seem to bring with them each year. You can count on those changes coming, but you never know with certainty just what they'll bring because they're never the same, are they?" He lifted his head, and looked out the window beyond Theo, as his gaze passed by him if not through him. "Whenever I do think about God—and I do—it's like that; that's how I think about him—constant, but ever changing, full of surprises, some exciting and some challenging, and others, well, frightening. That's how I think about God, like the seasons of the year."

Nurse Howard appeared in the doorway with her hands tight against her rounded hips. "Well," she said, "let's see how you two did this time!" Wagner had eaten just about everything on his platter while Theo managed the veggies, but hadn't really touched the chicken. Lifting the platter from his table, Nurse Howard offered her unwelcome assessment, "Listen Mr. Cross, you'll never regain your strength eating that way. My God in heaven, you already look like a sparrow. Eat man, eat!"

Theo thought about the word "sparrow" in the teaching of Jesus; something about not even a sparrow falling to the ground that God didn't take note. But he'd no taste for food and hadn't in months. It wouldn't change, unlike Wagner's seasons; Theo Cross would never regain his taste for food.

Nurse Howard picked up his tray and walked from the room with heavy steps. She returned and repeated the exercise with Wagner's tray. Theo felt somewhat relieved that she hadn't badgered him further about his appetite and his eating. He'd really try to eat tomorrow—even without taste.

In his upright position Wagner began to doze-off quickly. Theo wondered if it was because of the meal or because of the conversation they'd had over dinner. The thought passed away, and once more he gazed out the window.

The snow continued to fall; only now it was much heavier than before. "I guess Jessica won't be able to come for a visit this evening," Theo whispered to himself. Again he thought about the children, but this time his own grandchildren. Maybe they'd gone sledding after school. He'd always enjoyed going sledding with the grand kids when the hours weren't being devoured by more pressing, pastoral concerns. Theo thought about the snow falling softly on his shoulders and how his daughter, Jessica, always kidded him about having dandruff. A small smile crossed his lips and faded away just as quickly, like snowflakes melting on a warm windowpane. Without knowing why he was suddenly thinking about the seasons of the year, about changes, surprises, and God. Sometimes exciting, sometimes challenging, wasn't that what Wagner had said? He never thought about God in quite that way before this. It'd make a good sermon title; God and the changing seasons of life!

Nurse Howard was back in the room leaving her cart of medications standing just outside the door. "Time for your meds, both of you" she said. Pouring out some fresh water from a plastic canister and handing Theo his medications she admonished, "One at a time Mr. Cross." Nurse Howard then encouraged Theo to get some much needed sleep, "You've those treatments in the morning, and you know how they always wipe you out." She moved over to Wagner's bedside, nudged him on the shoulder, and extended to him both water and the same advice. Wagner took his meds and rolled on his side, returning to sleep. "Lights out now," she said, returning to her cart and moving on to the next room.

For the longest time Theo lay there staring at the ceiling tiles. In the dim light entering the room from the hallway, he could barely see the cracks. He had a crazy thought, or maybe it wasn't all that crazy after all. "Maybe death is like that," he thought to himself; "Maybe with death we no longer see the cracks in life, just darkness. Maybe that's all there is, just darkness and no longer seeing the cracks."

Each night, ever since his first year in seminary, Theo Cross offered a prayer before slipping into sleep. Sometimes it was long, with petitions for friends and family; sometimes it was shorter, with a simple thanksgiving for the day and the delights of the day—those unexpected, surprising delights. Tonight Theo prayed: *Ever changing God, full of surprises—some exciting, some challenging. Your love for all who suffer is constant. In your great mercy, help all who suffer, like my friend Wagner, give to each the strength to cope with their pain, hardships, and disappointments. Please bring sleep to sleepless eyes and peace to restless hearts and souls. And Lord, help me to change tomorrow, and to accept whatever changes you bring into my life. Grant me the grace to embrace your great surprises. Amen.*

He closed his eyes and thought about God and the changing seasons, and when he could no longer bear to think about God, he slept, but only for awhile, never for long. With Theo Cross—and with the exception of his love of God—nothing ever lasted for long.

2

Adequate Answers

Theology starts . . . with exploring the intersections between my story and God's story. It includes bringing to the surface the deep assumptions I've already made about who God is and testing them against the four sources of Scripture, tradition, reason, and experience.

It involves . . . formulating ever more adequate answers.

PHILIP CLAYTON

THEO HAD SPENT HIS years in seminary learning from some of the most brilliant minds in theology and biblical studies: Karl Barth, Emil Brunner, Rudolf Bultmann, the Niebuhr brothers. He'd been schooled in what was called "neo-orthodox or dialectical theology" by some, a "theology of crisis" or "kerygmatic" theology by others. What he'd learned would remain with him for the entirety of his career in pastoral ministry; what he'd internalized was more the value of disciplined study and biblical reflection, than allegiance to any one "school" of thought.

Theo was a good pastor, a devoted spouse, a caring parent, and one of the better theologians among his peers.

He loved the Church, he loved the work of ministry, and he loved the world in the way he believed a disciple of Christ was called to love the world—with respect for its broken-ness and regard for its place in God's plan of redemption. Yet all of this "love" was grounded in his love of God and, what he often called, the "things" of God. His colleagues would call on him to cover for them during vacation, be-cause, as they so often said, "Theo will bring the full mea-sure of God's Gospel to every act of pastoral care!"

He was also a realist when considering the church; he knew the church to be both the *communio sanctorum* and the *communio peccatorum*—a community of "saintly-sinners." But he also believed the church to be the last and best hope for the world, a world that had become increas-ingly more troubled in the years Theo had served in the pastorate. He'd seen people become more isolated, lonely, and left to themselves in times of distress; he'd seen the church become the target of unfair criticism from those who knew little or nothing of her nature and purpose; he'd grown tired of seeing the homeless treated with heart-less indifference by many of the very same people who expressed a disbelief in the virtues of Christian faith and doubted the existence of God.

Once more, Theo studied the dark contours of those cracks in the ceiling tiles above his bed and considered the coming fate of the man in the bed beside him. Had it been light, he would not have felt the freedom to do as he did there in the darkness. He wept, silently, for Wagner. And for Theo, his tears were the final prayer of the day. Again, he wandered off into semi-sleep, pseudo-death.

Theo was certain he wasn't dreaming when he first heard the voices. "Move the gurney closer Sam; I doubt that we can move him comfortably from this angle." On open-ing his eyes Theo found that he was gazing into the dark eyes of a lab technician, hanging over him like a buzzard over fallen prey. Theo found the young man's face pleasant enough, with eyes that seemed to dance to the rhythm of his cheerful voice. "Morning Mr. Cross," the technician said in tones that soothed the anxiety Theo was suddenly feeling, "You're scheduled for your treatments this morning, right?"

The helper was a rather large man, older than the technician and reminding Theo of the professional football player he once had as a member of his church. He was dark skinned, maybe fifty-five or so, with dark hair and a silence Theo found troubling. Since he didn't say a word, Theo wondered if his voice would be as large as his physical frame. Taking hold of Theo the technician first attempted to lift him on his own. When that failed, his helper, Sam, placed his immense arms under the shoulders and beneath the knees of the patient and gently lifted Theo to the waiting gurney—almost as if he were little more than a child's rag doll. At one time in his life, and not so very long ago, Theo weighed-in at close to two hundred pounds; now the combination of cancer and chemotherapy treatments had laid waste to his body, while at the same time testing the depth of his faith. Covering the patient with a sheet the technician pointed the gurney in the direction of the open door.

Wagner was just waking from a deep sleep as the gurney wheeled past his bed. He said, "Good luck Pastor!"

Theo wondered to himself what "luck" had to do with any of this, and in particular these discomforting treatments. His father had a favorite saying whenever someone spoke of luck. He'd say "Luck is for losers! Faith in God is all that really matters." Wanting to be polite Theo replied, "Thanks, I'll see you later—I suppose." With that the gurney exited the room and came to a stop at the nurse's station. The technician requested the patient's chart, and when in hand, simply placed it at the foot of the gurney. Soon they were once again on their way.

Moving down the corridor the wheels of the gurney jiggled out a peculiar kind of rhythm. Theo fixed his gaze on the ceiling tiles above as the gurney traveled at a good clip down the corridor. Then the craziest thought entered his head; he thought about how, in the past year, he'd spent so much time on his back—looking up! Theo wondered if maybe God wanted him to spend time on his back—flat on his back—dependent on others—even more dependent on God. All things had their place and all places had their importance in the providential plan of God. This was the eighth time in a year he'd been hospitalized; each time becoming somewhat more difficult for him and more draining on his family. Over the past year Theo had lost most of his appetite and some of his faith.

Theo Cross had large brown eyes, so dark they were almost black. Doris, his wife of almost thirty years, had always said that her husband's eyes reminded her of a child fascinated with the wonders of life—"wide-eyed wonder," she'd say. His face was small, which of course made his eyes appear larger than they actually were. He had jet black hair with just a hint of gray at his temples. His hairline gave him the appearance of being older than his age; people were always surprised to learn that he was only in his fifties. He'd always been reluctant to share his age with strangers and with the members of his church. Doris said it was vanity, while Theo argued it was merely his wish to maintain some privacy in a profession that called for outlandish candor. He often said that pastoral ministry had placed his family in a fish bowl of public scrutiny.

From the moment the technicians had removed him from his bed, Theo had begun experiencing a peculiar pain in his chest. He tried to relate this unfamiliar pain to some of the more common pains he'd experienced with his cancer and treatments. Theo thought this pain worse than a toothache but not quite as bad as being sawn in two! Grasping the hand of one of the technicians, the one who'd been informing him about the nature of the treatment he was about to undergo, Theo squeezed his hand so hard the technician winced in a pain of his own.

"What's up with the grip?" he said, "What seems to be the problem Mr. Cross?"

"A pain," Theo squeezed out, "a pain I've never felt before."

"Where's the pain?" the young man asked, "In your abdomen or in your chest?"

Pointing to the exact spot on his chest, Theo replied, "Here, just about—here!"

"No problem, don't worry Mr. Cross," the young man said through a slender smile, "We'll be sure to mention it to the doctor. Try to relax, we're almost there."

Understandably Theo wasn't in the mood to "relax" when what he wanted was attention to the pain, and to get the next treatment over with as soon as possible. He wanted to get over the sickness, the nausea, and the treatments. To hell with relaxing! The pain in his chest grew worse each minute and Theo wanted only for the pain to stop—*now*— not later. Just at that moment, they reached the double doors to the treatment center. The doors slowly opened automatically; finally the gurney bearing its load of skin-and-bones-and-a-new-kind-of-pain came to rest beside a huge piece of equipment the hospital used for such treatments.

Immediately a doctor appeared behind Theo. Peering down at him from that position, "Any complications?" he asked the technicians.

"None to speak of," answered the young man.

Theo turned to face the young man, "What about the pain? Remember the pain in my chest?"

The doctor turned to young man asking, "What pain is that?"

While fiddling with the pens in his breast pocket the technician said, "On the way here Mr. Cross indicated he was in distress, some discomfort in the chest area. Isn't that right Mr. Cross?"

Theo wondered why it was that these medical personnel would always translate "pain" to mean "distress" or "discomfort." Looking up at the doctor he said, "Not distress and not discomfort. Pain— right about—here!" Theo said once again pointing to the exact location.

The doctor just stood there, as if he'd just lost the capacity to speak. Taking out his stethoscope, he gently placed it beneath the loose fitting front of the hospital gown. "Well, let's have a listen, shall we." No alarm could be read on the doctor's face; no concern seemed to surface either. "Have you ever had heart trouble Mr. Cross," asked the doctor, "or is this the first time you felt this particular pain in your chest?"

Theo shook his head, "No, never before."

With a shrug of the shoulders the doctor removed the stethoscope and walked away. Not a word; not a grunt; not so much as a peep. Nothing! And the pain only grew worse. Then there was silence and peace; deep, deep rest from the pain—escape.

When he awoke, Theo was back in his room, in his bed, beneath the ceiling with all of those random cracks; again he began thinking about his life, his pastorate, his long life of service. Suddenly there came the thought—as if spoken by some distant, yet all too familiar voice, whispering in his ear—"It's time to write your story, Theo. It's time."

Theo reached into the drawer of the night table beside his bed, took out the composition book, reminding him of sometime from his childhood—some time lost to memory, or at least to his immediate recall. He also grabbed the pen from the drawer and wrote on the first page: "The Life and Times of Theo Cross." Scribbling those words, he dropped a line or two and wrote: "A Pastoral Memoir." He scribbled out those words also. Dropping down to the middle of the page, he wrote: "Forever: A Pastoral Confession." Theo stared at the last phrase, wondering where in the world he was supposed to go now. "It's time." Well, perhaps, he thought to himself, but what was he to "confess?"

Confession was the singular act Theo had always associated with sin and faith, yet couldn't think of any reason why he should write some extended narrative as a confession of either his innumerable sins—to the extent that he could remember his sins spread out over the length of a lifetime—or even a confession of faith, since so many others had done so, and done so with an eloquence he lacked. He thought about the one confessional narrative he'd read and re-read hundreds of times over the years. St. Augustine's *Confessions* was, to Theo Cross, without equal. He held pen to paper, as if waiting for some mysterious muse, perhaps even the spirit of Augustine himself, to prompt the initial words—words that would contain enough charisma to grab the attention of anyone who might dare to read his narrative. Nothing came, just the blank page staring up at him, as if to taunt him to write something—anything. Nothing came, except that still, small voice saying over and over again, "It's time."

Then, it happened. It happened just as it had on countless occasions. There were those strange moments when, in preparing his sermon, there came this mental block, more a void than a blank. Theo would sit, sometimes for hours, listening to Mozart, hoping that the Holy Spirit would burn through his study with a flame sufficient to set ablaze his slumbering imagination. As God would have it, at least according to the theology of Theo Cross, as *God would have it*, there came a glimmer of insight that soon erupted into a blazing inferno of imagery, bringing to life a word that was as good as dead, a kind of resurrection, the breath of new life—and for an hour or more, he'd write without stopping. Sometimes when he'd stopped writing, he'd read the text and wonder where in the world such ideas came from with such astonishing clarity and insight; certainly not from his intellect, his memory, or his life-experiences. Theo never thought himself a creative person, but a quite average preacher, with limited writing skills and insufficient experience in life for the creation of any truly helpful illustrative material. Whenever these moments of awakening came, he was certain it was from beyond him, beyond and above, above and arrayed in spiritual light. Preaching plagued his heart and soul; he loved preaching, and yet often discovered preparations to be tedious to the point of being insufferable, all in the same breath. He yearned to speak the unspeakable; he longed for his lips to be burned with hot coals from some biblical altar, brought by an angel with tongs, touching and torching his words, even as they took shape on paper. "It's time. It's time. It's time."

How he had managed to get from his room to the treatment center, back to his room, and then back to the treatment center once again was one of those mysteries for which Theo would never receive an adequate answer. He could, however, recall that last mysterious message: "It's time." Still the question haunted him; time, for what? Theo was amazed that he should be witnessing the young technician and his huge counterpart walking into a back room, a room from which they emerged almost as quickly as they'd entered it. Looking to another who was behind Theo as he lay on some cold table, the young technician said, "Everything is ready doctor whenever you are."

Doctor Mears hadn't been the attending physician at the treatments Theo had already undergone, but he seemed to Theo a nice enough person—although his skill as a physician was still undecided, at least as far as Theo Cross was concerned. As the treatment proceeded Theo attempted to focus on something else, a way of avoiding this unpleasant experience which was nevertheless essential to his present survival. From some direction Theo couldn't determine he heard the doctor ask him how he was feeling.

"I believe this pain is getting worse," Theo said through clenched teeth. Finding it increasingly difficult to breathe he added, "And I can't seem to catch my breath!"

"The pain—is it still in the same area?" the doctor asked.

Theo moved his right hand to his chest area, saying "It's tight, really tight—tighter—I can't breathe; I can't . . . !"

Scrambling for his stethoscope, and while placing it over Theo's chest, he heard but a faint rhythm—a beat, beat, beat, like a drum retreating into a distance. Then silence—nothing—like—death.

Mears cried out to the technicians, "Sam, Jim, get the hell over here—stat! Sound code blue for Christ's sake!" Immediately the treatment room was filled with people all working frantically, like ants over a lump of sugar. Theo was still, silent, unresponsive to the attention being given his body.

Theo was elsewhere, somewhere far, far away from that place, that time, that business all about his physical frame—motionless. He'd been given a ticket for this trip in a thought that came to him just before he lost consciousness; it was a remembrance, making present the conversation he'd had with Wagner. Theo remembered that he was once a Roman Catholic; not that he'd ever forgotten that fact, but this thought came now with a revelation, a remembrance; making present once again some profound and misplaced memory.

He was maybe eight years of age—nine at most—a time when he loved the neighborhood in which his family lived, with numerous friends, open fields, and plenty of time for play! The neighborhood seemed to Theo to have been made with children in mind—well-kept yards, big trees just made for exploration, flower gardens galore, and an ice-cream parlor within biking distance. There was a baseball field just two blocks from his house where every Saturday Theo, his two brothers, and their friends would gather for a game.

Like all of his friends, with the exception of those strange kids who attended some Protestant church, Theo attended the local Catholic school. Theo's friends all attended St. John the Divine R.C. Church, and both Saturday evening "confession" and Sunday morning Mass were mandatory—even when interrupting the more important matters of childhood play. Theo's older brother was an altar boy and a favorite of Father James who was always challenging Theo to "measure up" to his brother—"Guy." Everyone called him "Guy," though Theo never discovered the reason why. Even though there was a significant difference in their ages, Guy was good to Theo and welcomed him to come along whenever Guy would "hang out" with his own crowd. Theo and his younger brother—Dan—now that was another story altogether!

Even as a child, Theo seemed to possess a certain "power;" at least that's what his friends were always telling him. They didn't use the word "power" but would say things like, "Theo, God really hears your prayers," or, "God listens to you more than He does any of us; you're special to Him!" And even though he wasn't all that certain he wanted the responsibility that attended such high esteem for his relationship with God, Theo relished the way such adulation made him feel—a kind of prominence mixed with a measure of fear and dread that he'd be in big trouble if he ever did anything to displease God.

And what if it weren't true? Theo would charge his friends not to say such "silly" and "dangerous" things about him—to make claims he'd never consider making of himself. Still, somewhere in the dark corners of his mind he wondered if they might not be right, that he actually had a very special place in God's plan—whatever that was. After all in catechism the nun taught about those special people in the Bible and Church called "saints," who had a really important part to play in God's plan—whatever that was. There were people like Moses, David, and the guys who were with Jesus before they got scared by the cross and all of that messy stuff. Weren't they all just normal guys before they were told that God had a role for them in His plan— whatever that was? And if them—why not *him*, and if then, why not *now*?

It was very early on a Saturday morning, much earlier than Theo was accustomed to getting out of bed, and in particular on the one day when he could sleep in. The knock on the door was familiar only because it was the secret knock of his best friend, Junior. Stumbling to the door and opening it, Theo found Junior in tears.

"What's wrong?" Theo asked as Junior brushed by him, making his way to the large couch in the far corner of the living room—the only piece of furniture facing the TV.

"It's Teddy," Junior said through a voice strangled by more tears, "He was hit by a car last night and he's dead."

Theo sat next to Junior, offering what comfort he could, "God, Junior, I'm really sorry. Teddy was always running across that damn road, and never once looked in any direction; just—bam—off and running across the damn road!"

Junior, wiping tears from his eyes, glared at Theo, "Damn you Theo! My cat isn't to blame for some stupid ass driver not watching where he was going. Don't blame Teddy! Maybe I should be blaming that God you're always talking about—how about that?"

Theo leapt from his spot on the couch, moving closer to the door of his parent's bedroom, where they were still sleeping. "Wait a minute, pal," said Theo, straining not to shout at his best friend—or worse still—wake his parents early on a Saturday morning, "you just caught me by surprise, that's all!"

Theo stood while Junior sat—both in silence for a long time.

"Look Junior, I'm sorry. I can see that this is really tough for you. I never had a pet like Teddy, so I don't know what to say or even how to say what should be said when some . . ." Theo caught himself, "some*one* dies so suddenly!"

Junior lifted his head, looking at his friend through more tears, and taking one of the throw pillows to his chest—as if hugging Teddy. Then, Junior said, "I didn't come just to tell you, Theo; I came to ask a big favor of you as my best friend." Standing and then moving ever so slowly in Theo's direction, Junior said "Dad dug a kind of grave in the backyard, near Mom's garden. Boy—she loved that! Anyway, it's not a grave like the Catholic cemetery, with crosses and statues and other religious stuff, but Dad made a cross from two sticks and stuck it at Teddy's head; I mean—where Teddy's head is in the grave." Another long silence, and then he said, "Maybe you could come and say one of those special prayers you say. You know, the kind that will reach God and make Him welcome Teddy—you know—home or in heaven—or whatever?" With that, Junior returned to the couch and sat in the nest-like spot his oversized pre-teen body had already created.

It wasn't so much the request that startled Theo, as it was what Junior said once he'd returned to the couch. Looking at his best friend he said, "Oh God, Theo, I just remembered! You don't think it'll matter to God that Teddy isn't buried in one of those Catholic graves, do you? I mean, good God, we haven't been to Mass in like a century. I don't think that priest would even know who we were if we did show up some Sunday."

Theo smiled and said, "I don't think that priest would know who you were if you attended every Sunday for a century!" Moving over to take a seat next to Junior, Theo went on to say, "Look buddy, I doubt that any of that kind of stuff matters much to God—like where someone's buried, or what kind of stone or whatever marks the grave. What matters to God is how you live and the way you treat other people. As far as I could tell Teddy was a good cat who loved you a lot and never caused you any grief—I mean—before this thing."

Reaching out to touch Junior's hand for the first time since he'd arrived, Theo said, "Maybe you should just pray for Teddy yourself. After all, he was your cat, and I think that would matter to God, because you'd kind of be saying 'thanks' to God for Teddy. You know what I mean?"

"I don't know," answered Junior with tears coming to his eyes for what seemed to him like the umpteenth-zillionth time, "I'm sure God won't hear my prayer—I mean listen to me."

"But why?" asked Theo.

"Because," Junior said, again reaching for the throw pillow and pulling it to his chest, "my mom says that God won't listen to people who pray when they've done bad things. And I stole some of my dad's tools to fix my bike and I lost them—I don't know where the hell they are! See, there I go again, cursing!"

Turning away from Junior, Theo was thinking about the time he'd stolen something of far greater value than some tools, and he'd never told a soul, not even the priest in confession. It was his secret sin, between him and God. Wanting to extract himself from this conversation as quickly as possible, and before his best friend noticed his guilty expression, Theo replied, "Look Junior, I'll come by and pray for Teddy. But I got to tell you—I'm not sure God will listen to me anymore than He'll listen to any person who did something bad or wrong or whatever—yourself included. But, I'll come because I'm your friend."

When they arrived at the house Junior's mother was out in the garden doing some last minute planting, and apparently tending to the freshly dug grave of the late Teddy.

"Hello," was the only greeting Theo could come-up with; every kid in the neighborhood including Junior!—knew that Theo had a "huge crush" on Junior's mom.

"Oh, hello there, Theo. Have you come to comfort Junior and to pay your respects to little Teddy?" she asked as she tended to a renegade wisp of hair, placing it behind her ear in a way that just about sent Theo into cardiac arrest.

"Kind of" was all Theo could muster, as he was still in some far off fantasy land.

Junior was staring at the mound of earth in the garden and the crude cross that marked the grave of his late pet. After picking up her garden tools and while heading for the back door of their house, Junior's mother called, "Don't be too long Junior, we've got the doctor's appointment at 11:30."

Junior and Theo stood motionless and speechless over the freshly dug grave. Theo reached out to nudge Junior on the elbow, motioning them both to their knees, saying, "Listen, I'll say some things and after I say, 'For all these things' you say 'Lord, hear our prayer.' You got that, right?" Junior nodded his head in assent, nervous that he might blow the whole prayer if he got it wrong—but there it was!

After a brief pause and the noise of a jet passing overhead, Theo began: "God of all the pets and things that make kids happy, for all these things," and Junior added, "Lord, hear our prayer." Taking a breath, Theo continued, "God of all small things and big things, of all the joy and all the sadness, of all the life and all the death, for all these things," and Junior responded, "Lord, hear our prayer." Thinking about Teddy and Junior's earlier tears, Theo went on to say: "God who loves us and cares about the things that make us sad and lonely, for all these things." There was an awkward silence. Theo glanced over at his friend, his best friend. Junior's shoulders were shaking and Theo knew he was weeping, but trying not to disclose his pain. Taking Junior's hand, and now while wiping tears from his own eyes, Theo said, "Lord, hear our prayer."

Theo was suddenly, unexpectedly thinking—remembering—the way the priest had prayed at his grandfather's funeral. Gently he added, "God, take Teddy—even though he was only a cat—into heaven with you, or wherever pets go after they die, and watch that he doesn't cross any highways there in heaven; for all these things," and Junior sighed out "Lord, hear our prayer."

It was then that something occurred, shocking Theo, actually jolting him. Junior reached out and took the hand of his friend, his best friend, and held it in a vice grip. Theo then finished the prayer saying, "God, help Junior and his mom and dad to feel better, not to be so sad, and to know that Teddy is doing okay with you—wherever that is—and that you love them too, for all these things," Junior responded so quietly it was barely audible, "Lord, hear our prayer." And with that, they were done.

Junior's mom called from the back porch, "Junior. It's almost time to go!" Junior said good-by to Theo, and getting to his feet ran to the back porch.

Theo remained on his knees, staring at the grave, wondering what in the world had just happened, and why he was the one to speak that prayer, and where the words came from, and why it was he felt lighter than before—like he felt after removing a ton of outer garments in the winter. He rose to his feet and headed for his bike, resting against the railing of the back porch steps. Junior's mom was waiting there, and as he mounted his bike, she thanked Theo for his friendship with Junior and for the prayer. Theo was speechless, but only because he just couldn't break his contact with her eyes—he loved her eyes.

Theo made his way home, taking his time and going by the local playground to see if any of the guys were there—but they were probably all at the local matinee, a Saturday treat! Peddling away from the playground Theo thought about Teddy and death and graves and prayer. He wondered if God really listened to prayers and if He did— why? He wondered what Teddy would look like in heaven and what his grandfather would look like in heaven. He wondered what heaven would look like. Prayer and God and graves and—death!

Suddenly Theo felt a tightness in his chest—a kind of panic. For some inexplicable reason he was suddenly thinking about the thing he'd once stolen, frightened that maybe God didn't listen to his prayer for Teddy after all. Theo thought adults knew more about such things than did kids, and Junior's mom did say that God doesn't listen to the prayers of people who do bad things—and stealing was pretty bad! Strange how it is with kids. Thoughts come and go—like phantoms, like ghosts—haunting your mind instead of someone's house. As quickly as this troubled remembrance had come, it was gone—gone well beyond Theo's ability to retrieve. Theo thought that maybe he and Junior could go fishing the next day, but only after Mass, of course. Then there was that fear again, that panic, causing Theo to shiver. "Fishing," it had something to do with "fishing." His father's best fishing pole and tackle—that was the "stolen" thing; that was the act that could cause his prayer to pass by God like a guided missile; his father's favorite rod and reel. Remembering is sometimes the most painful thing a kid can do.

Even though just a kid, Theo knew that when the priest in the Mass used the phrase spoken by Jesus—"Do this in *remembrance* of me!"—he meant more than just remember his name, face, and stuff like that. Theo always considered those words somehow different from any others spoke in the Mass, or in prayer, or anywhere for that matter. His grandmother used to tell him that when the priest spoke those words it was calling their attention to a "presence," and even though she never told Theo exactly what that "presence" was—he seemed, in his gut, to know that Jesus was there, then, in some strange way.

Theo imagined that for the first followers of Jesus that kind of remembering must have been really painful, what with the cross and all of that suffering Jesus went through. Maybe some kinds of remembering can be both, Theo reasoned, both painful and somehow good—that was the only word he could come up with—good. Perhaps it was also "good" that he remembered the "stolen" rod and reel; a "good" that wasn't yet clear, but maybe would be some day.

3

Steal Away

Do not steal.

(DEUTERONOMY 5.19)

THEO FOUND A PARTICULAR joy in Friday evening meals. As "practicing" Catholics his family would not eat meat on Fridays and so his mother always prepared Theo's favorite—tuna fish hoagies with French fries and iced tea, topped off with strawberry shortcake. Theo always told his friends that his mom's tuna hoagies were "to die for" and that any other fish dish would be a joke in his household on a Friday. His older brother, Guy, was able to eat at least three of his mother's hoagies at a sitting, something Theo thought impossible, but there it was in his face each and every Friday—one after another after another after another! And that didn't include the huge pile of French fries Guy could also put away. Theo used to say he swore Guy had a hollow leg or was like a cow with several stomachs. Friday was one of the more casual meals in the household and even Theo's grandmother—who was forced to live with them after she lost her husband and her home—even she would sit before the TV with her tray of food. It was the only time when the family didn't sit at the dining room table. So, for Theo, Friday evenings were the best.

On this particular Friday evening Theo had a pressing question, and one that he was certain would be answered negatively—at least by his grandmother who, as an Irish Catholic would never tolerate the children missing Mass, even if Mom and Dad chose to sleep in on Sunday mornings. "Mom, Dad," Theo asked pensively, "can I go fishing with Junior in the morning—I mean Sunday morning?"

Simply shrugging her shoulders his mother said, "It's alright with me, just so you come home in time to finish that homework."

Theo's father, on the other hand, was silent for the longest time and then said, "Just be careful son, you and Junior tend to get in all kinds of trouble whenever you put your two boney heads together!"

Theo watched as his younger brother polished off his hoagie in what seemed like two bites, devouring his meal as if it were the last dinner of a condemned man. Turning his eyes to his father Theo dared to ask, "Dad, can I use your new rod and reel?"

The look he received in return was his answer: "Absolutely not!"

While pushing his plate aside his father took Theo's forearm in his large hand and said, "That's a very expensive piece of equipment; it took your mom all of her tips for six months to save enough to buy that rig for my birthday last spring. Besides, your mom and I just gave you a new rig of your own for Christmas—use that."

Saturday came and went with little or no excitement in the neighborhood and more than a few really bored kids as a consequence. Saturday night Theo made certain to set his parent's alarm clock for 4 a.m., as the best time for fishing was early morning, and he and Junior wanted to beat all of those Protestant kids to the best spots on the stream. Not able to fall asleep, Theo was thinking about his father's comment and command—but still couldn't get that beautiful rod and reel of his dad's out of his head. He longed to have it in his hands. Remembering his grandmother's comment that "stealing" was against the commandment of God, Theo prayed, "Lead me not into temptation; lead me not into temptation—please God— no temptation!" After a lengthy stretch of pleading Theo gave up on praying and returned to the more pleasurable fantasy of his father's fine fishing rig!

On the night before a "fishing trip" Theo would sleep in his clothing, reasoning that it would take far less time in the morning to get out of the house and to the stream. A punch in the arm was what awakened Theo and not the alarm. His brother was pounding on his arm, "Come on, you jerk, it's four in the morning—get the hell out of here! God—you are such a pain."

Theo rubbed his aching arm, got up, laced up his sneakers and headed for the garage and his bike. On his way to the garage and from the kitchen window, Theo saw that Junior was waiting on the back porch. Junior was smaller than Theo, much too heavy for his height, with tiny plump fingers on each hand and a face as round as a roll; yet for all of that, even as a kid, Theo knew that junior had—what he called—a good heart and soul. Gulping down the last bit of milk in the glass, and pointing Junior toward the garage with his finger, Theo said, "Let's get going before the fish stop biting!"

Entering the garage from the house, as Junior came in from a back door, Theo went immediately to the place where his father kept that wonderful fishing gear—that "expensive" rod and reel. He knew it was wrong to take it; he knew it was "like" stealing; he knew that his mother had worked long and hard to provide it for her husband; he knew all of that and more—still—the temptation had finally gotten the best of Theo. Quietly lifting the rod and reel from the special perch his dad had made for the gear, Theo handed it to Junior. As if it were contaminated, Junior jumped back at first, saying "I'm not touching that thing! As neat as it is—your dad will kill me if I touch it or drop it, or some stupid thing."

Theo held it in his hands, pointing the tip of the rod upward as if preparing for a long cast. And then he did the unthinkable; he took the rod and reel and walked to his bike, sat down on it, and began to peddle away. It was so alarming to Junior that he just stood there at the entrance to the garage, unable to move a muscle. Then he hopped on his bike and sped off in the direction Theo had taken—toward the stream.

When the boys arrived at the stream they made their way to their favorite spot. It was a small stream, running through pasture land, with large curves and cut out banks, and some very deep pools for its size. Their favorite spot was beside an old oak tree with a high bank and a deep pool that had been formed by the spring flood waters surging through that stream over years. Just beneath the bank the water was exceptionally deep and the current stronger than in most other areas of the stream—even at the widest sections. Junior had once measured the depth by putting a sinker on of a piece of ribbon and dropping it into the water until it finally came to rest on the bottom of the stream bed. While they never determined the exact depth, they both knew that whatever went into that portion of the stream was never going to be retrieved—in particular by them!

Theo and Junior set up their fishing gear, each placing a fat worm carefully on the hook, casting into the fast water, allowing their lines to come to rest on the sandy bottom of the stream. Junior always brought food in a paper bag; he said that the fresh air always made him hungrier than usual. Theo laid his father's rig on the bank, at the very edge, so that the line would hang free over the water—better to see when a fish would strike the bait. Turning his back on Junior, he walked a short distance away, beyond the canopy of leaves provided by the old oak, to look up at a bright blue sky. Junior ate one of his sandwiches, then another, and finished off the third. Remembering his mom had put a piece of chocolate cake in the bag, he reached into the bag with his fat-little-fingers—pushing the bag away from him as he did, and not noticing the bag drifting away—he hit Theo's father's rig and sent it into the water below.

The splash of the rig hitting the water startled Theo. Turning toward Junior, he saw that his dad's "expensive" fishing gear was nowhere to be seen! Theo cried out, "God, no! What have you done you oversized jelly donut. Are you insane, or what? Aren't you fat enough already without bringing food here?"

Jumping to his feet Junior shouted, "What the hell, Theo! We'll just use my line and get your precious rod and reel back again!"

For one flash of a moment Theo felt relief; maybe they could retrieve his dad's gear from the water after all. But that moment passed and Theo was left with a feeling of absolute dread. They tried for an hour before it became apparent to them both that the rig was gone—maybe even flushed away to the sea and the locker of the late Davey Jones!

Grabbing Junior by the front of his shirt, tearing it at two of the button holes, Theo wrestled Junior to the ground, "You big fat jerk! You knew that was my dad's gear—you knew it was expensive—you knew it! Now what? My dad is going to slaughter me!"

Pushing Theo back, almost to the edge of the bank, his head hanging out over the water, Junior cried, "Look, you're the one who stole the stupid rod and reel! Don't blame me for what happened, when that stuff shouldn't have been here in the first place—you stole it!"

With that Junior picked up his rod and reeled in his line, and having picked up what remained of his brown bag lunch, jumped on his bike and raced away for home.

Theo watched as Junior crossed the open pasture, until his small rounded frame fell over the far horizon and onto the macadam—and Junior was gone. Theo thought that Junior was right, he'd "stolen" his dad's gear and it had no place with them that day—it belonged to his dad and should have stayed where it was in the garage; it wasn't his and his dad had made it clear that he should use his own gear. But he also felt bad for having blamed his friend—his best friend—and for getting so angry only because he knew that Junior was right and he was wrong—from the beginning, he was wrong! So now—what was he going to do?

Getting to his feet and brushing the dusty dirt from his jeans and shirt, Theo started to walk his bike through the pasture. He attempted to pray, to ask God to forgive him, but it just didn't seem to Theo to be a genuine prayer; after all he brought all of this on himself! Then Theo remembered the prayer he'd been taught when he was very little. Every time he lost something important, his mom would tell him to pray to St. Anthony—the patron saint of lost causes—and so Theo prayed beneath his breath: "St. Anthony, St. Anthony, please come around. Something is lost and can't be found. If it is found, bring it to me, and I will thank thee." He repeated the prayer numerous times on his bike ride home, wondering how some saint in God-knows-where would find the fishing gear, retrieve it from the deep waters, and finally "bring it" to him at home. It all seemed like too much of a miracle to possibly happen—especially since this "lost" item was actually "stolen!"

Evening came and Theo took note that his dad was later than normal; his dad took Sunday afternoons to play golf with his buddies, and they all went to the local VFW afterward for a few beers and a game or two of darts. Theo spent the time—from his arrival at the back door to the moment his mom called him to the dinner table—in his room, thinking, praying, hoping against hope that his dad would forgive him for having "stolen" his prize fishing gear. He heard the front door close and then his dad's voice in the kitchen, and then—and then—the door to the garage open! Panic set in immediately. Silence was long and torturous. Theo overheard his dad say something like "where is it?"

Panic like he'd never known before in his life—even the panic felt when the "wolf" that used to hang out in his closet at night would appear, growling and bearing its teeth at him, long after everyone else in the house was sleeping! Relief only came when he heard his mom say, "It's beside the refrigerator in the corner." It was only then that Theo *knew* the missing item *wasn't* the "stolen" item.

At supper Theo watched his father and noted that he hadn't said one word during the whole of the family meal, which was highly unlike his dad. Even Theo's mom must have noticed his extreme silence because she said, "John, is everything alright with you? Is there a problem or something?"

Theo's dad simple shrugged his shoulders as he said, "No." But Theo sat bolt upright in his chair as his father continued, "When I pulled into the garage this evening, I noticed that my rod and reel were missing." And turning his face in the direction of his son Theo he continued, "Does anyone know what happened to them—to that beautiful gift Mother gave me—the one that she'd worked so hard and so many hours to purchase? Anyone here know where the fishing rig got to?"

Pushing his face deeper into his dish Theo felt that all eyes at that table were now fixed on him—and he was right! He took a deep breath and said, "I don't know Dad, but maybe St. Anthony will find the rod and reel."

At that point Theo's mom lashed out, "What are you saying, Theo? How could you show such disrespect for your father?"

Theo waited for some word from his dad. There was none to come, just a look on his dad's face that Theo had never seen before this—one that he would never forget.

After dinner Theo headed to his bedroom. An hour or so later his dad knocked on the door and upon entering said, "Is there something you want to tell me son?"

It was as if someone hit a button in the heart and soul of Theo Cross—he burst into tears and confessed the whole tragic event, from the theft to the loss in the murky depths of the stream! But what was most amazing of all, Theo did not even mention Junior; instead he took all of the responsibility. As he was about to learn, that was a very smart thing to do. Looking squarely into Theo's eyes his dad said, "I'm not okay that you took and lost that fishing gear, and you'll work your paper route to make it up to your mother and me, but I am proud of you for being truthful with me."

That was the sum total of the accountability; no punishment, no harangue, no scolding or what would be worse—spanking with the belt! His father said his piece, turned, and left the room. It was one of those childhood experiences that Theo Cross would bear in memory for the rest of his life. He'd remember his father's face, voice, gestures—but mostly (what he would later come to call) *grace*.

Never again would he "steal" anything—nothing so much as a paper clip! It wasn't the loss of the rod and reel that taught Theo Cross the most important lesson in life, it was the fact that his dad—the one who felt the loss more keenly—had forgiven him and while still holding him accountable for its replacement, teaching Theo to show respect for the property of others and for his mother's gift of love to her husband.

This was to be the first but not the last time that Theo was to encounter the powerful force of "*grace.*" Not as some abstract term, but as a flesh and blood reality; a force that changes someone in a profound way to be, almost inconceivable; a force that is felt in and through the human heart and soul.

One Spring day, two years after the tragic event of the loss of the "expensive" fishing gear, Theo and Junior—now two years older and, as they thought themselves, *wiser*—went fishing at that same stream. As they walked the banks after their attempts to catch, well, *anything*, they rounded a bend in the stream, and from the height of the bank on which they stood, they saw it. It was still intact, though rusted. Theo stared at the gear, and turning to Junior said, "I guess St. Anthony has his own time for finding lost stuff!" It was, though not as powerful, yet another expression of *grace*.

Theo took the gear home, and as he handed it to his father, his dad said with a smile, "Well, I'll be damned! And all these years I thought that 'St. Anthony' stuff was just so much horse manure!"

———◦———

"Mr. Cross? Mr. Cross? Come on, wake up, Mr. Cross!" Theo opened his eyes and immediately recognized the cracks in the ceiling above; he was back in his room and in his bed. He also couldn't help but notice the extra wires attached to his chest and the IV inserted in his right arm.

His wife, Doris, and eldest daughter, Jessica, were standing to the left of his bed, looking pensive—at best. There was another doctor at his right—one he'd not seen prior to this occasion; his nametag read "Dr. A.W. Mitchell."

"What happened?" Theo asked in a raspy voice, "I don't remember anything. What happened doctor?"

"I called your wife and daughter because of the seriousness of your condition."

"What condition?" Theo asked—"You mean my cancer?"

Theo turned to Doris, "Honey, what condition?"

Doris said, "Just relax and let Dr. Mitchell explain, please."

Dr. Mitchell stepped behind Doris and Jessica and pulled the pink curtain around the bed for a semblance of privacy. He took his position at the foot of Theo's bed. "Mr. Cross, you had a heart attack or to be more exact, congestive heart failure; in laymen's terms, when sufficient amounts of fluid build-up around the lungs, it can cause the heart to give out. Don't worry, we have the situation under control, and with significant rest, medication, and monitoring of your condition, you should be fine for now. I'll be keeping a close watch." Dr. Mitchell gave a short smile to Doris and Jessica, pushed the curtain away from the bed, and left the room.

Doris ran her delicate fingers through Theo's thinning hair. Looking intently into his eyes, she could see that he was deeply concerned. Trying to reassure him was difficult, only because she was aware that the cancer was terminal and time limited, and reassuring Theo regarding this recent heart attack wouldn't be much reassurance at all.

"Theo, honey," Doris said softly, "it seems the treatments led to this heart attack—and if we continue any treatment, there could be another, or worse. The cancer has spread too far for them to do much more. I think we need to talk about your," tears interrupted her for but a moment, then she whispered, "your *death*."

Strange as it will seem to some, Doris and Theo hadn't previously discussed his death, even when it became crystal clear that this cancer was terminal. The very thing that Pastor Cross had often discussed with others of his congregation, he couldn't bring himself to speak of—even though death wasn't what he feared most; what he feared more than death was pain, and leaving Doris and the family.

But now there just wasn't enough time to mince words and worry about feelings, this conversation was a necessary one—regardless of the difficult nature of what could be shared in such a short amount of time. How does one cram nearly thirty years of marriage into a few weeks of shared remembrance? How do you say all that needs to be said when the clock relentlessly pushes on to the inevitable end? What more can one do than hold on and hold out for some shred of hope against hope that . . . .?

Doris turned from the bed and Theo and walked over to the window, gazing at the newly fallen snow. "We had another snow fall Darling. Did you know that?"

Theo was staring at the ceiling above, "What? What was that you said Doris?"

She turned, "I said, we had another snow fall. The children really seem to be enjoying it."

Jessica located the opening in the curtain and exited the room without saying a word to her father. From the corridor came the faint sound of crying—It was Jessica. Theo looked into Doris' bright blue eyes, so deep, he often said, he could swim in them for an eternity and never reach the depth of her heart and soul.

"Honey, do you think Jessica will be okay? I'm worried about her. You know how fragile she is with situations like her father being—her father—dying."

Reaching out and taking his hand in her own Doris counselled, "Listen, don't worry so much about Jessica. She's stronger than you think and able to deal with almost anything. Think about yourself for once. Save your own strength; keep your strength for all that you have to face, okay?"

Doris leaned over the bed rail and planted a long kiss on Theo's mouth. "You try and get some rest now Sweetheart. We'll see you tomorrow, I'm certain." Their eyes met and for one brief moment they faced the truth together in the love they'd shared for so many years; it would be an act of sheer *grace* to have more.

Theo pulled Doris close enough so that he could whisper, "Sweetheart, I'm crazy in love with you—even after all these years!"

A small smile broke the corners of Doris' mouth as she said, "No, Theo, you're just plain CRAZY! Now, get some rest, please."

As Doris pressed her hand to Theo's chest, and as she turned to leave the room, Theo caught the faint smell of his favorite perfume—passion welled up in his heart, as if he were twenty again, and he desired to hold his beloved wife in his arms, just once again, just them, flesh on flesh. "This at last is flesh of my flesh, bone of my bone."

As Theo heard Doris speaking with Jessica softly outside his room he offered a simple prayer beneath his breath: "*God of all grace, bless my family with the emotional and spiritual strength needed to meet the weeks ahead.*"

Before she left, Doris pushed the curtain back to the wall, and for the first time Theo noticed his roommate, Wagner, wasn't in his bed. When the nurse came in she said, "You gave us quite a fright Mr. Cross! Don't do that again, please."

Gazing at the nurse adjusting the lines to his monitor, Theo asked her, "Where's Mr. Wagner?"

She turned and looked at Theo as if he'd asked the question in a foreign language, saying "I'm sorry, what did you just ask me?"

Theo pressed his head into the pillow, as if to back away from her words in shock, "I asked you where my roommate, Mr. Wagner is?"

In what could only be called a cold monotone, she replied, "I'm sorry no one told you, Mr. Cross; Mr. Wagner died last night." As she straightened his sheet at the foot of his bed, Theo thought he detected a slight clouding of her eyes, "You try and get some rest" she said, "if there's anything you need, anything at all—just buzz."

As she headed for the door Theo, called, "Wait, please, wait. I was wondering if you could do something for me."

Returning to his bedside with a look of curiosity the nurse replied, "Of course, Mr. Cross, what would you like?"

Theo thought for a moment and then said, "I'd like to offer a prayer for Mr. Wagner and his loved ones, and I'd appreciate your help if it's not too much trouble."

Looking into his face the nurse replied, "No trouble at all—what would you like me to do?" Theo asked her to respond to each petition of his prayer with the words, "*Lord, hear our prayer.*"

Theo began: "*God of the changing seasons and of our ever changing lives, we praise you for your incredible grace, for this and all else,*" and the nurse responded, "*Lord, hear our prayer.*"

Theo continued: "*God of summer, fall, winter, and spring, the birds of the air, beasts of the field, brother sun and sister moon, for this and all else,*" and again came the response, "*Lord, hear our prayer.*"

Theo went on to pray even more fervently: "*God whose ever constant and faithful love enables us to deal with the painful and distasteful changes in life, enables us to accept the silences and uncertainties of life, and enables us to continue to hope for the renewal of life, for this and all else,*" and the nurse responded, "*Lord, hear our prayer.*"

Now Theo thought about Wagner's family: "*God of surprises—some exciting, some challenging, some frightening—help our brother's family to live with his death, to accept the winter of their loss with hearts set on the spring of your resurrection,*" now wiping tears from her eyes and without being prompted, the nurse whispered, "*Lord, hear our prayer.*"

The two were very still; still and silent. Seeing that Theo was weeping silently, the nurse finished the prayer, quietly, "*Amen.*"

After whiping the tears from Theo's eyes, the nurse smiled and said, "You're a *good* man, Pastor Cross. My pastor would say that you're a minister of *grace*. Now, please, get some rest, and don't get me in trouble for keeping you from the rest the doctor has ordered!"

After she left the room, Theo thought about Wagner, his sense of humor, their first conversation, his understanding of God—like the changing seasons of the year—wonderfully unpredictable! Theo realized—maybe as he'd never realized before in his life—that others can teach even the most seasoned pastor to think about God in more expansive ways, with deeper and more profound considerations than many of those many dry tomes of theologians. But what he thought about even more was the way in which even Wagner—a person he'd known for such a short span of time, with little knowledge of his loves, dreams, and desires—this man had been like a touch of *grace*, simply because he'd provided Theo with a lovely image of God.

Theo had always found it difficult to let others—family or friends—get really close to him. He often reasoned that this was because there was little room in his heart for both God and too many others. It was merely a rationalization, but that's what he told himself when he found himself alone in his office, his study, or his living room. And yet, somehow this all-but-total-stranger named "Wagner" had found a place in the heart of Theo Cross. That too, Theo mused, was *grace*. He even wondered what Wagner would look like in heaven!

Then, suddenly, a pinch of anger: "Why did they revive me if they know I'm dying anyway? Why not just let me go? Why revive a man with a rope around his neck?"

Night fell, as did his spirit, and Theo Cross cried himself to sleep—first anger; then fear; then tears; then, at long last, sleep.

4

Death Never "Takes a Holiday"

*Lord of life and conqueror of death, you are our help in every
time of trouble. In the presence of death, you comfort those
who mourn. We bow before you, believing you bear our
grief and share in our sense of loss. Give us grace to worship
you, and to trust in your goodness and mercy. Assure us that
because Christ lives, we shall live also . . . God of grace and
power, send your Holy Spirit among us, that we may hear your
promises and know them to be true, and to receive the comfort
and peace they bring; through Jesus Christ our Lord. Amen.*

*BOOK OF COMMON ORDER
OF THE CHURCH OF SCOTLAND*

IT MUST HAVE BEEN the middle of the night when Theo
awakened with a start; without a watch he judged the time
by the shades of light and darkness in his room, and even
more so by the activity of the nurses on the floor. Theo
wasn't sure the exact thought that awakened him like a bolt
of lightning. He felt pain, but not the pain associated with
illness—with cancer. His pain was far more emotional; he
was thinking again about Wagner, and if there'd been an

attempt to revive him, and the relief from pain associated with his death. What troubled Theo most about that fact was that the "relief" came to Wagner only at the cost of his life. Death. Once more Theo was thinking about death and graves and God—and yes, freedom from this suffering and pain, but at such an immense cost. Why was it, that after all these years of development in medical technology, death remained the definitive answer for release from the devastating pain associated with this particular disease?

Theo watched through squinted eyes as a shadow crept along the wall in front of him, like some mysterious phantom. Was death some form of shadowed existence?

Theo prayed: "*Even though I walk through the shadow of the valley of death, I will fear no evil—for Thou art with me.*" It was one of the more powerful metaphors in the work of the psalmist, and one that Theo believed as much as he did the teaching of Christ in the gospels. Suddenly the question returned to him—as if spoken to him, as if whispered in his ear: "Why did they revive me?" This time around the question expanded: "Doesn't anyone understand that I was so close to freedom, delivered from this horrible pain and suffering?" A cough from one of the distant rooms echoed down the corridor. He thought about Doris, Jessica, the nurse—and *their* tears. Theo thought about Wagner, and how they must've made the effort to "revive" Wagner. As quickly as he'd been awakened, Theo fell back into a deep sleep, into yet another dream.

Dreams are this peculiar mixture of past and present, as characters and events from the past and present merge, making a shared appearance on the stage of the dream-drama. Dreams transcend all barriers of time, place, and even common sense. The dream is no respecter of barriers established by the conscious mind; the walls of time, place, and circumstance all collapse. The last conscious thought before drifting off to sleep often becomes the director, actors, and plot of the dream-drama about to unfold—unfolding, that is, before the watchful inner eye of the heart and soul. On this night, at least for Theo Cross, the thought was no more than a word, but a word that was haunting him—"revive!"

Theo was sick with the flu and home from school—restricted pretty much to his bed and bedroom. He'd never minded staying home from school—what kid doesn't at age 12!—even though the ticket was a sickness that made life almost unbearable. Staying home provided time to work on his models—which were primarily models of birds of prey. On this day, the model was that of an owl. He'd completed the construction in his spare time and was now running a fine brush with the exact color over the contoured feathers—as if to bring the bird to life! Theo loved owls in particular because, as his mom once told him, "They are the wisest of birds." But, at least according to his Irish grandmother, who seemed to have brought Ireland and all of its mystery with her to the States, "These creatures also have a dark side"—she said, "They bring death to the house, whether hooting outside a window or making a home within—like that model of yours!" His grandmother even attempted on one occasion to throw the model in the trash. Fortunately Theo's mom saw her and later retrieved the bird before any further damage could be done. The day Theo and his mom had purchased the model at the toy store, his mom had momentarily objected warning, "Theo, not an owl; remember what my mother told you—bad business those owls!" In maternal love, she relented, and they came home—all three—the mother, son, and the owl!

From his bed, and while he was placing the finishing touches on the down feathers of his owl, Theo heard a knock at the front door, and then two distinct voices, one familiar—his mom's—and the other a male voice. All he

49

heard clearly through the door to his bedroom was something about a telegram. The front door closed and there was the sound of an envelope being torn open, and then, "Oh my God! No! No! Oh God no—Dear Lord in heaven—Oh, sweet Jesus—No—Not him—My God not him!" Theo heard a loud thud coming from the hallway, and then silence. He knew it must have been his mom falling to the floor. Theo, still holding the model in his hands, was frozen in place by a panic that was far greater than he'd felt the day the "stolen" fishing gear hit the water. His knees began to shake uncontrollably.

Finally Theo jumped from his bed, dropping the model to the floor, and ran down the stairs. At the foot of the stairs lay a torn envelope and what must have been the telegram. Picking up the yellow paper from the floor, Theo's eyes fell on the heading, "Western Union." Now the sound of sobbing was coming from the kitchen. Lifting his eyes from the yellow paper, he saw his mom in a pile on the kitchen floor.

Theo's eyes returned to the telegram, which read:

> DEAR MR. AND MRS. CROSS: IT IS WITH
> DEEPEST REGRET THAT WE INFORM
> YOU THAT YOUR SON, AIRMAN SECOND
> CLASS WILLIAM P.D. CROSS, WAS SHOT
> AND KILLED WHILE STATIONED AT
> MISSLE SITE #442, MYERS AFB, TOPEKA,
> KANSAS. EVERY EFFORT WAS MADE TO
> REVIVE YOUR SON. A REPRESENTATIVE
> OF THE US AIR FORCE WILL ARRIVE AT
> YOUR HOME WITHIN THE WEEK. WE OF-
> FER OUR DEEPEST SYMPATHIES.

Limply walking into the kitchen, walking as if he'd been shot, Theo staggered to where his mom was still on the floor, sobbing, and cried "Mom? It isn't true, say it isn't right, Guy can't be dead, just can't be! He was just home! Mom, Mom—please—tell me this is wrong, a mistake or something—please!"

His words simply stopped at that point and there was only one thing to do; Theo dropped to the floor, sobbing as he took his mother in his trembling arms. God only knows how long they were on the floor sharing in tears before Theo bolted upright and said, "Mom, what should I do? Should I call the priest, call Dad? What Mom, please, what do I do?"

Picking herself up off the kitchen floor and whiping the tears from her eyes, Mrs. Cross picked up the phone and dialed the workplace of her husband. Already her eyes were red and swollen and a deep darkness had settled over her face, so that Theo barely recognized her. As she spoke to her husband she choked out every single word. "Hi, honey," she started slowly, "we've received terrible news, dreadful news. I—I can't—I can't . . . ." She dropped the phone receiver and then followed it to the floor, collapsing in a pool of pain and tears.

Theo picked up the phone and without thinking what he was saying, simply said—as if he were telling his dad that the furnace had broken down, or the front door fell off its hinges—"Dad, Guy's dead—this telegram we got says that he's dead!"

The next voice Theo heard over the receiver was his father's boss, "Theo, your dad's on his way home. You watch your mom. He'll be home soon."

Then silence and a feeling completely unfamiliar to Theo, a feeling he would come to know again the day his doctor told him, "There's nothing more we can do; it's just a matter of time."

Theo reached out to comfort his mom, as she trembled like a kitten left in an ally on a cold winter's night. He could no longer keep back his tears. His mom grabbed Theo by the arm, almost yanking him out of his clothes, and pulled him so close to her he had trouble breathing. As if she were informing some unseen person, Theo's mom said, "He's dead, he's really dead—gone, we'll never see him again, ever. Why? Why would God do such a thing? Why be so cruel and why him? Why? What did I ever do to deserve this?"

Theo tore himself from his mom's grasp, flew up the stairs to his bedroom, found the owl on the floor where it'd fallen when he jumped from the bed, picked it up, and, with all the force of his being, threw it against the wall. That wasn't sufficient! He jumped on the broken pieces until the model was unrecognizable—nothing more than a pile of twisted plastic. The same rage he had just before witnessed with his mom, now exploded from within Theo. He spoke to the mass of plastic as if it were a best friend who'd betrayed his trust. "You stupid thing! How could anything so beautiful do something so ugly? You're not wise at all; you're a coward; you're just a coward. You bring death and then fly away—free. I hate you; I'll hate you until I die, too." Like his mom on the floor below, Theo collapsed, sobbing.

If not for the knock at the front door, Theo would've simply stayed glued to the floor, to his guilt, and to his grief. He jumped to his feet and rushed down the stairs, almost falling flat on his face. When he opened the door Theo recognized the figure immediately, even with his back to the door; it was Father Murphy. "Where's your mother, Theo?" he said while stepping through the doorway. "I received a call from the base chaplain and I know about Guy—that's why I'm here. Your father stopped at the rectory—he's not far behind me. Now, where's your mom?"

Theo led Father Murphy into the kitchen where his mother was now seated at the kitchen table, holding a dish towel to her face. The priest first put his arms around Theo and bent to whisper in the boy's ear, "Don't you worry now, Theo, it'll be alright." Then he stepped over where Mrs. Cross could see him.

His mother's eyes were even more swollen than previously, Theo placed his hand on her wrist and waited for a reaction, but there was none—none at all.

Mrs. Cross fixed her gaze on the priest and pleaded, "Father, why? Why was it Guy? Our boy's dead and I want God to tell me why this happened. And if he can't, I need you to make sense of this whole God-awful-mess!"

Taking her by the arm, Father Murphy gently led Mrs. Cross to the living room and the large couch, while Theo followed behind, slowly—silently. Sitting next to her on the couch, Father Murphy took a deep breath, released a deeper sigh, and replied, "I don't have such answers; I don't know that anyone does; and I doubt that God sees Himself as accountable to us and the questions such tragic and incomprehensible losses bring in their wake." The priest took her by the hand, "But that's not why I'm here, and you have to know that. I'm here to offer whatever comfort and strength I can. We all loved Guy and feel this horrible loss—not in the depth you and your family feel it—but it has touched us all."

It was at that point that Theo's father entered the house by the garage door at the back of the kitchen. Falling to his knees, he buried his face in his wife's lap—together, they wept a long, lonely weeping. Gently patting the grieving father on the shoulder, Father Murphy offered, "If it's all the same to you both, I'd like to just stay here in the house— with you and the family—at least for the next several hours." Neither parent said anything in response, but Father Murphy took that as confirmation he should stay—which he did—for hours.

Theo Cross

All the rest of the day the house was buzzing with people: friends, neighbors, family members—all coming to express their sympathies. Some came with empty hands and hearts filled with pain, a shared sense of loss; others came with hands filled with food or flowers or both, and with hearts empty of any sense of sympathy—it was more like curiosity.

At one point Theo looked at his mom and dad and thought, "They look like tears had stained their faces with sadness." A strange thought came to him; he wondered if his mom and dad would be like the clay model he'd once made—soft in the beginning, but then hardened into a set form, with his fingerprints still visible on the unyielding clay. He wondered if his mom and dad would be similarly hardened in the sadness now covering them; this horrible loss of his brother leaving fingerprints of death, still seen on them, in some indescribable way—forever.

After receiving a phone call, Father Murphy had to leave. He went first to Theo's parents, and then came to Theo and said, "I'm so sorry for your loss. Please come and see me if you need anything at all."

Suddenly it occurred to Theo that he hadn't seen Dan. The entire time—from the moment Dan had arrived home under the direction of the Principal who had told him, "Dan, there's been an accident. You must go home!"— to the leave taking of Father Murphy, Dan had been sitting under a tree. Looking from the kitchen window, Theo saw him leaning against the tree in the backyard. As was so often the case, he sat alone. Dan was as different from Guy as night from day; he was darker, more sullen, less sociable, and quick tempered. But Dan had a gift that was unique to him; he saw and had this sensitivity for—what could only be called—"beauty" in the world, and he was able to capture that "beauty" in his drawings and paintings. Even so, Theo always felt more comfortable approaching Guy than he did Dan. But now Dan was the only brother he had. Theo felt compelled to go and see if Dan wanted to talk. He didn't!

Back in the kitchen, Theo overheard someone say, this terrible and tragic death "must have been God's will." Although he couldn't make sense of it, he was beginning to wonder if death wasn't the "tool of God" to take people from this life—even the smallest of children. He wasn't about to tell anyone about the owl, wondering how a little plastic model could possess such great power that it could be the cause of his brother's death from hundreds of miles away! He remembered a comment, once made by one of the nuns, that God created all things, and all things can be used of God for His own divine ends—His own reasons. Would that include the model of an owl, a silly piece of plastic? Would God use his own creation for the destruction of life? Was death like the "right hand of God" he'd heard so much about in catechetical instruction? Is it absurd to think that God created owls simply as instruments of death? Then the deeper, darker, more troubling realization came to Theo. His newly discovered hatred of owls was beginning to take shape as hatred of *God*!

As more and more adults made their way into the kitchen to prepare a meal for those who could eat—certainly not Theo's parents!—he ventured into the living room. There he found that yellow telegram, and read again how they'd attempted to "revive" Guy. Theo just couldn't make sense of what such an attempt would look like, and in particular since Guy had been shot. His thoughts were dark—painful, but he couldn't stem the flood of thoughts: "Did Guy suffer? Did he scream out? Did he bleed and bleed and bleed? Was Guy frightened? Did he have any idea that he was dying, and if so, what was that like? Was it like falling from a tree, or was it more like slipping into sleep?" His thoughts were finally interrupted by the touch of a hand on his shoulder. It was his favorite uncle, the one for whom his brother was named—Dan.

Gently removing the yellow telegram from his hand, his uncle said to Theo, "Come on Theo, it won't do you any good to read it again. How are you holding up?"

Beginning to cry Theo said "I just can't stand being here. I can't stop thinking about it. And I'm scared to death it's my fault. That stupid model. Why did God create those stupid birds? All they do is kill people—I mean, bring death into the house!"

Wide-eyed and completely baffled, his uncle asked, "What in the name of God are you talking about, Theo?"

Pulling out two chairs in the dining room, they sat side-by-side in a corner.

"Grandma always says that owls bring death to a house."

"Okay" said his uncle.

"And I was working on the model of an owl when we got the yellow thing about Guy getting shot and dead."

His uncle pulled his chair somewhat closer to Theo, saying, "Okay" I get that—but what has one to do with the other?"

Theo looked at his favorite uncle as if he had six heads and wondered how he couldn't have seen the connection, so with a tone of sarcasm he tried again. "I was working on the owl; Grandma says that owls bring death, and Guy's dead!"

His uncle lifted both hands in the air, as if he were reaching for a butterfly in flight, "Oh, now I see! You are responsible for Guy's death. Is that it?"

Theo jumped to his feet, "Not so loud! Of course that's it!"

Taking Theo by the hands, his uncle gently pulled the boy back down onto the chair. His uncle's face had grown serious, even somber, "No son, it's not your fault; your brother's dead because he was shot by some lunatic trying to breach a secure fence that he was guarding. That's always the risk of military service—your life's on the line, period! Guns are dangerous in anyone's hands, even the best trained. It's not about some model and it's certainly not your fault that we're feeling this pain."

Noting that Theo's thoughts were drifting off in some other direction, Uncle Dan said, "Look, Theo, your grandmother means well, but she still believes some pretty silly things—superstitions and such. That's all they are—just stories that try to make sense of what is otherwise senseless. Do you understand?"

Theo found his uncle's voice comforting, but his words less than credible. He thanked him, stood up, and retreated to his room, again stepping on pieces of plastic as he crashed onto his bed—crying—sobbing—alone and lonely.

———⋅◦⋅———

October passed into November and November into December, and there'd been two serious snowstorms in less than a week. It was dark, with a deep snow covering the ground around the gate to the cemetery—snow that piled high. As Theo opened the gate to enter, he wondered if he would even be able to locate the grave under the cover of all the snow. The only light came from a distant street lamp, which cast a dull yellow glow over the pristine snow—reminding Theo of the yellow telegram and its terrible message. His family had already been to the grave on numerous occasions, but always without his mom. She once said to Theo's dad, "I'll not see some mound of earth that's swallowed up our son! I'll never visit that place of death—there's nothing there for me." On this occasion, Theo decided he needed to come alone—facing "death" as if facing a lion in the arena in Rome. (Yes—he'd read about the early martyrs of the Christian faith!).

As Theo entered the cemetery—the first time through this particular gated entrance—he was surprised to be greeted by a large statue of the Virgin Mary, the "Blessed Mother." The yellow glow from the street lamp gave contour to her face and seemed almost to animate this lifeless piece of stone. Theo first noticed the small smile breaking at the corners of Mary's mouth only as he struggled to make his way past her. The smile caused him to pause; to glare; to wonder what this woman had to smile about—if anything. The smile seemed to him a kind of smirk or the smile of one of the girls in school who, on having some stupid secret about him, would simply gaze at him with this cat-that-swallowed-the-canary grin. And Theo wanted to know what it was—if that was it—what it was she was up to and what did she know?

Bracing himself against the frigid night wind, Theo looked intently into Mary's face. "You're the worst person I know! See, I know something too!"

Tears came to his eyes, but the air was so cold they literally froze on his cheeks; "You and that stupid Son of yours, and that God who kills people! Why don't you just leave us humans alone for Christ's sake? If all you're going to do is bring death and then smile about it—well—the hell with that!"

Suddenly there was a rush of shame and guilt, which came and left as quickly as the winter wind biting at his open skin, "I hate you—all of you---wherever you are, and I'll never trust you again—ever!"

Theo tried to pack snowballs to toss at Mary's image, but the snow was too powdery to pack tightly. He dug beneath the deep snow, found some small stones, tried to scratch them lose until his hands could take no more—and gave up on the effort.

Theo felt his shame, guilt and anger churning in his mouth, like snow with sleet. "You're a witch—do you hear me? You're nothing but a witch in a blue dress, and I absolutely detest you, your Son, God—all of you for killing Guy—for taking my brother—for making my mom sad beyond belief!" And then he remembered the word "revive." Suddenly the anger became an emotional tsunami, "God-damn you all! Why didn't the revive thing work? Why didn't you do for Guy what you did to those guys in the Bible? What the hell is wrong with you? Don't you love us—really? Do you really hate us and just pretend to love us because it makes you look good?"

The wind picked up, blowing so hard against Theo's back it knocked him to his knees and he was all but buried in the deep snow at the foot of the statue of Mary. Looking up he saw two things he'd missed before this: Mary's arms were open, like his mom's whenever she wanted a hug from him, and there were, or what appeared to be, tears on her cheeks.

Theo remembered Calvary, the long week of suffering that the nuns had told them about each year during Lent. He remembered the death and the loss and Mary standing at the foot of the cross, watching her Son slowly, irrevocably, slipping from life to death. She was there the whole time; standing in statuesque form—unmoved by the shouting and vile taunting of the crowd—simply a mother present at the dying of her Son. The words welled up from Theo's heart and he whispered into the howling wind, "I forgot your pain; I'm sorry. Please, forgive me for saying such stupid things. I know you know how much we all hurt right now and how death can make you wonder what life's all about. I know you know what's going on in my heart. I'm really sorry and I'll never forget again—I promise."

He felt the chill come over his entire body as he'd now been out in this brutal winter storm for far too long. Theo pulled himself to his feet and gazing at the statue one more time said, "I'll be okay; I think now I'll be okay."

Theo turned and walked away from the statue, the cemetery, the superstition, and from the face of death—death as the face he'd learned to fear. He wasn't certain what it was he understood; he simply knew that he felt somehow different—stronger.

A heavy snow continued to fall on the long walk home, and Theo was certain he would deal with the storm, with God, and with death. Making his way along the unshoveled sidewalks, Theo thought, "Life is strange—all that belief stuff is strange—death is—well, it just is—but *God*?" As he turned down his home street he suddenly stopped dead in his tracks, because the thought was all but paralyzing. Theo dared to whisper the strange question beneath his breath and into the dense, cold night air, "Did God try to revive His Jesus, or is that what they mean— something like what they mean when they talk about—what was the word?—oh—*resurrection*?"

Dreams end as quickly as they begin, with no thought given to time and place. They come and they go like phantoms in the night—shadows drifting across the wall. Yet they always leave something behind—a feeling, a thought, a memory—something that remains with the dreamer, long after the curtain has come down on the dream drama. Theo slowly opened his eyes to a new day. He couldn't remember the content of the dream; he only knew that he felt stronger, and he was even more certain then he'd been in the past that he would deal with the storm-of-sickness, and with God, and—yes—with *death*.

5

Hospitality to Strangers

Don't neglect to show hospitality, for by doing this some have welcomed angels as guests without knowing it.

HEBREWS 13:2

THE HOSPITAL LOUNGE ON the fourth floor was decorated in bright yellows and blues; soft chairs and a single couch, with one coffee table laden with magazines left the large room looking odd—as if the message conveyed were something like: *Enjoy the stay, but don't get too comfortable!* A television was suspended from the ceiling in one corner, emitting a constant barrage of infomercials and other inane programming. Doris Cross entered the lounge and sat in one corner, on the only couch available, noting immediately that she was the room's sole occupant.

Doris seldom wore casual or "street" clothing, preferring to dress in a way that presented an air of professionalism. This day she was wearing a two piece dark blue suit, softened by a decorative scarf; her hair, as always, was perfectly in place. For whatever reason, Doris had always been extremely conscious of her appearance. Like her husband, she believed that the first impression was always the most important.

Doris was a clinical psychologist, with her own office and a very successful practice. She actually had so many clients she needed to constantly make referrals to colleagues to avoid overextending herself. Theo would look to Doris for professional insights whenever the issues facing a member of his congregation exceeded his limited training in pastoral counsel, and her advice was almost always incredibly insightful and helpful to the process of resolution.

Over the years, Doris had gained a reputation for being one of the best therapists in her field in her state. She was proud of the fact that other psychologists often sought her counsel on their more difficult cases. She was also a part-time professor at a local university teaching no less than three courses each semester. Some of her articles, in particular those on her favorite area of therapeutic care, dealing with dependency and addiction—were published by the more prestigious academic and professional journals.

Doris' practice had been—ever since Theo was first admitted to the hospital—to come to the hospital at least one hour before going in to visit him. As she put it, she needed the time to process the events of the day prior to the visit with her husband. It sounded so "clinical" even to her own hearing, but this ritual enabled her to cleanse her mind—and often her heart—of the stains left behind by dealing with no less than fifteen clients on any given day!

Since she was alone in the lounge, Doris turned off the TV just as *Moon River* began to play over the sound system. It was a song that took Doris back in memory to the senior prom and the first time she'd danced with Theo Cross. They knew each other since they were in grade school. Doris' father was the pastor of a large Presbyterian church in their neighborhood, and he'd always encouraged his only daughter to form friendships with members of the several churches in their immediate area. *Moon River* had become the traditional last song for the prom, and as she and Theo danced, he kept drawing her closer and closer, until she said, "Any closer and I'll be behind you!" They'd felt a strong and mutual attraction throughout high school—a love that hadn't yet matured, but would grow and deepen while they were in college and away from each other.

"Do you mind if I sit beside you?" The question awakened Doris from her day dream; the song had ended several minutes before. The young man posing the question was tall, with dark hair and hazel—somewhat intense—eyes. Although he was dressed casually, Doris felt that he had about him the "air" of a professional.

Gazing into those hazel eyes for the first time, Doris repled, "Yes, of course, please."

Seating himself on the couch beside her, he extended his right hand and with a broad smile and introduced himself: "Hello, my name is Jim O'Connor."

Somewhat taken by surprise Doris said, "Hello, I'm Doris Cross."

Pensively, the young man thought aloud, "Cross, Cross. God that name is familiar to me. You're here to visit someone, are you?"

Holding her palms flat on the lap, Doris replied, "Yes, my husband; he's been in for several weeks now—cancer."

Placing his arm on the back of the sofa, Jim softened his tone, "And how serious is his condition—if that isn't too intrusive a question?"

Casting her eyes to the floor Doris thought for a moment and answered, "The doctors have determined that my husband can no longer tolerate the treatments and so—well—there's little they can do but keep Theo comfortable. I doubt that he's ready to face his inevitable death, but I trust in his strength and spirit to face it with courage and dignity when he's ready."

Doris wondered why it was she could speak so freely with a total stranger. This was the first time she had confided in anyone about Theo's condition and prognosis. She wasn't one to talk so candidly about "family matters," but it seemed so easy, somehow safe to talk with this young stranger. She noticed how he listened to her with genuine concern evident in those intense eyes.

Doris had always enjoyed meeting new people and hearing them recount their experiences, lives, vocations, and families. Yet somehow, for some inexplicable reason, this time and this young man were different. She was insightful enough to know that the attraction wasn't physical so much as it was emotional; she wanted, and needed, to share Theo's illness and imminent death with someone other than family—as they were always, and understandably, reluctant to open themselves to her expressed pain and struggle.

Turning to face Jim directly Doris admitted, "This is the first time I've felt comfortable enough to share all of this—and with a stranger at that!"

Jim smiled and said, "It's often the stranger who provides the safest place for sharing our pain."

They shared in one of those awkward silences that can arise at such moments, and then Jim was the first to speak, while Doris listened intently—as if to one of her clients. "Sometimes it's easier to speak of such matters with a stranger because, unlike family, a stranger usually has no investment in offering advice, or counsel, or trying to resolve the issue expressed." Noting that Doris wasn't going to comment, Jim continued his monologue, "Family can be a great source of comfort and strength, but they're also close to the situation, to the pain and suffering of the loved one and that alone makes it difficult for them to listen. It's not that they don't care, it's just that they're struggling with their own emotions and standing on the very same battlefield."

Jim fell silent. Doris reached out, touching his shoulder with professional concern. Then coming back from wherever it was he'd traveled in his memory, Jim continued, "I recall when my grandmother was dying of an excruciating cancer. The rest of the family kept these long hours of silence—like a vigil. We couldn't talk about grandmother's pain or her death. I remember the evening I was alone with her in her hospital room, talking with a person visiting the other patient. It was such a comfort—just to talk—to express those painful feelings, to a total stranger. So, I suppose there're occasions when it's easier, and better, to talk to a stranger—to share with someone who hasn't an emotional investment in your loved one."

Doris considered it amazing that such depth of wisdom could be found in such a young life. She recalled a sermon her husband had preached on several occasions in which he said that wisdom was a gift of God's Holy Spirit, and was no respecter of age or social standing—given only and always for the enrichment of life. She smiled to herself. She always thought his preaching exceptional, but she considered the sermon on "Divine Wisdom" to have been one of Theo's *better* moments in the pulpit.

Doris took Jim's right hand in her own. "I'm so glad we've had this chance meeting—and I'm grateful for your attention and sensitivity."

Jim locked his eyes on hers. "Maybe it's not 'chance' at all. I think that God has His own place, time, and purpose for bringing certain individuals together—His own reason for stranger touching stranger. Like the passage in the *Letter to the Hebrews*, which says something about being hospitable—open even to strangers—because you never know, the stranger could well be an angel of the Lord."

Bridge over Troubled Waters came floating into the lounge. Holding Jim's hand tightly, Doris said "I've always thought this would be a great song to add to a church's hymnal. It's such an inspiring piece of music, and the lyric is profoundly spiritual—don't you think?"

Jim cocked his ear in the direction of the music and agreed, "Yes, it is. Are you Christian?"

Doris watched the nurses and doctors and staff hustling about in the corridor just outside the lounge, "Yes, I am—it's all I've ever known—spiritually speaking. My father was a Presbyterian pastor and my grandfather and great-grandfather before him. My father thought that I'd enter the profession as well, but, that just wasn't for me. You're a Christian? I have to assume so by your reference to *Hebrews*."

Jim considered changing the subject, but thought that would be rude; instead he replied, "Born and raised in the Roman Catholic Church—or as my Irish grandmother would have put it—THE Church!" Doris found that she was becoming more interested in this young man with such sensitivity.

In all the time Doris had been coming to the hospital and spending time in this same lounge, she'd never before had anyone approach her, for anything—and certainly not to converse with her about her Theo. Previously she'd made professional contact with one of the chaplains on staff—the Protestant chaplain—and was told there was a Roman Catholic chaplain as well. So, where were they? To date, she'd seen neither of the chaplains. Jim had held her interest, and it had nothing to do with attraction; it was more like curiosity as to *why* he'd spent so much time with her and why he had expressed his concern for her and her husband with such sincerity and compassion. Even though she'd accepted his observation that it's often easier to speak with a stranger, such an observation would not account for *this* level of interest in her.

Without any prompting from Doris, Jim continued his narrative: "My father was a devout Catholic prior to the Second World War. He'd been selected for enrollment at one of the most prestigious Catholic universities in this country, but his mother and father couldn't possibly afford to send him. I recall Dad telling me about the experience, how deprived he felt having lost the opportunity of a lifetime. Anyway, after the war he came home and abandoned his Catholic faith altogether; Dad claimed to have become an 'agnostic,' but I always believed he was really no less than a closet Roman Catholic."

Doris smiled as Jim continued: "It's not that he divorced himself from any belief in God, but he had no stomach for—what he called—'organized religion.' He'd always close such testimony to his 'loss of faith' with the statement, 'I've seen humanity at its worst,' and it had literally torn the heart from his faith!"

Suddenly Jim was aware that he'd been speaking without interruption. "I'm sorry, how rude of me to go on with all of that!"

Doris countered, "No, please, I'm fascinated. Please."

Jim reached over to the coffee table. Picking up one of the many magazines, he leafed through it, as if looking for some article of interest—or maybe it was no more than a momentary diversion. "My mother," Jim continued, "now she's something else altogether! My mother seems to have maintained some form of faith or belief, though for the love of God I couldn't tell you exactly *what* it is: some strange mixture of Roman Catholic and cultural superstitions and agnosticism. She hasn't attended Mass in years; I can't recall the last time she went to Confession; but she still holds this bizarre belief in the intercessory power of the Saints!" He threw the magazine he'd been holding onto the table and selected another. "Her religious beliefs seem to come and go like the wind." Suddenly, closing and throwing the magazine back onto the table, he sat silently with a sullen expression on his face. Doris observed this change in Jim, but determined it best to avoid addressing it at all—on any level.

"I'm sorry Mrs. Cross."

After shuffling the magazines on the table, as if trying to rearrange them, but only randomly moving them about for what amounted to another distraction, he went on, "I get upset talking about my folks. I'd give anything to see them more proactively engaged in their Catholic heritage—but that's just not going to happen."

It was with the words "proactively engaged" that Doris began to see how this young man was distancing himself from his feelings and from his family.

"My father has a piece of the truth and thinks it's the whole of it," he explained. "My mother has the part that makes her 'feel good' or 'secure,' but seems disinterested in the weightier issues of Christian conviction. Do you know what I mean?"

As a clinical psychologist, Doris had learned long ago that there's great value in honest reply. "Frankly, no" she said, "I haven't a clue as to what you mean? Is it that you think they should never have left the Catholic Church in the first place?"

Jim fixed his eyes on the magazine table as if attempting to read one or more without opening the cover. His stare became fixation and his fixation became regression into memory.

When at last he spoke his voice was soft and slow, as if he were pondering each word—selecting each one with great concentration and care. "I think it would've been better for them to just wait out their spiritual storm—whatever it was—and continue their search for contentment of soul from within the Church. I've never counseled someone to leave the Church in order to explore doubts or misgivings about the faith. Sooner or later all Christian believers will become disenchanted with the humanity of the Church and with those aspects of her teaching and tradition that seem to them antiquated or irrelevant. Faith is always a journey along the pathway of highs and lows, joys and sorrows. It seems to me that the Church is, herself, a kind of troupe, a collection of those who are seeking an ever deeper connection with God—we're all 'seekers' of one kind or another. I wish my parents had remained within the community of the faithful, without settling for less—in the spiritual or soulful sense."

Jim lifted his face from his intense fixation and looked directly into Doris' eyes; what she noted was the intensity that radiated from his gaze. She thought about Theo—the intensity, the passion in his eyes whenever he would talk about the church, faith, and God. But that was years before, when Theo was a neophyte pastor, not yet fully seasoned in the paradoxes of the church.

Doris always thought that younger Christians had a way of wearing their faith on their sleeve, obvious to all, ever ready to enter into biblical or theological debate, they were eager to demonstrate their new found knowledge. They'd enter into the most controversial topics, like warriors in combat, without a thought given to sensitivity for the convictions of others. She remembered how energetic Theo had become as a young seminarian, tackling with intensity all of those perplexing and deep questions about the meaning and purpose of life, about God, Christ, and the church—about death and life beyond death. She remembered the serious conversations that would take place at table in the seminary commissary whenever she chose to join Theo and his friends for lunch. Her remembrances were interrupted by Jim as he continued his narration unabated.

"You see, Mrs. Cross, I love my Church—her teaching, tradition and institutions—because all have given greater meaning to my life. I wouldn't trade being Roman Catholic for 'all the tea in China'—as they say." Jim paused long enough only to watch as a mother and child walked past the lounge. "I mean no disrespect to your faith," he continued with a furrowed brow, "but for me the Roman Catholic Church is the one true Church—the one rooted in the Apostolic tradition."

Watching Doris closely for any sign of discomfort or even displeasure, Jim admitted, "I'm not like those who advocate that the Church must become more open to other religious beliefs and systems; for me that would eventuate in a sacrifice of all that's unique and beautiful to our own Catholic heritage."

Even though she was respectful of his candor, Doris felt that Jim was also very naïve, sacrificing some of his own natural wisdom to youthful enthusiasm. She wondered if perhaps he wouldn't mellow with age and would mature in pastoral office, learning to distinguish between concession and a genuine openness to other faith perspectives. Like Theo, Doris had always felt that the strength of the Christian faith was in its rich diversity of expressions, and that its greatest strength was in its capacity to compromise with and internalize the very best of whatever cultural setting it called home. Having met people from other Christian traditions who felt very much like Jim, she'd always thought them rigid. Doris, on the other hand, loved attending ecumenical conferences with Theo and the exposure it offered to the rich and variegated tapestry of the Christian heritage.

Doris decided to take advantage of the lull in the conversation. "Jim," she addressed him directly, "I'd like to tell you something about my husband. Perhaps it will be a new insight for you. Regardless, I'd like to share something." Doris placed her hands on her lap, fingers intertwined. "When my Theo and I arrived at First Presbyterian, the community expressed little or no interest in ecumenical affairs. I recall one of the first sermons he preached there; it was about the richness of the Christian heritage. Theo spoke so forcefully of the necessity for sharing with other Christians, so that we might come to a better appreciation of the beauty and vitality of Christianity."

Doris paused to see if Jim was still listening. He was, with rapped attention. Encouraged, she continued, "Theo always believed that one could come to a deeper understanding of his or her own tradition through open dialogue with those from another tradition, so he decided to begin an ecumenical study group with both ordained and lay people in attendance. It was exciting to see participants emerge from former prejudicial and stereotypical viewpoints to a much larger and more appreciative perspective. As it turned out, Theo was correct, and those who participated in the group also developed a deeper understanding of their own tradition as well. It proved to be one of the most important ministries among the churches of our community."

By the expression on his face, Doris could see that Jim was less than convinced. "I can appreciate all of that," he allowed with an air of borderline superiority, "but I still think it's best if we don't 'mix apples and oranges,' so to speak. Maybe it's good for people to have exposure to other expressions of Christianity, but I think many people just end up confused regarding what is best—what is the most orthodox expression of the Christian faith."

Someone entered the lounge, and without regard for Doris and Jim, flicked on the TV. Jim requested that she turn down the volume and then continued, "As a Roman Catholic I think it best that all Roman Catholics remain skeptical and cautious about dialogue with other Christian traditions—God only knows where such intermingling could lead in the long run."

Doris suggested, "In the long run—they could become far better Christians!"

Suddenly Doris thought of Theo, and a question he would ask came mind. "Jim, suppose you were a chaplain in this hospital and one of the patients—Protestant—requested the Eucharist, would you refuse him or her the Sacrament?"

Jim studied the faces on the TV in order to delay dealing with the question, but knew he couldn't avoid responding. "Well, yes, I suppose that's exactly what I'd have to do. The difference between sacramental theologies is still vitally important to Roman Catholics. I'd tell the patient I'd be glad to refer him or her to the Protestant chaplain—but that's all I'd be willing to do."

Doris then challenged him further, "And what if that patient were dying? What if you couldn't be certain time allowed for such a referral?"

Doris thought it strange that she would formulate a question in such terms; the words seemed to her to come from elsewhere—not from her own mind.

Jim looked at Doris with astonishment. "I'd still think it best not to administer the sacrament. I'd pray with the patient, but sharing the sacrament is another matter altogether. What's the point you're trying to make?" Jim asked. Doris noted a tone of annoyance.

Undaunted, Doris challenged again. "The point is that you're being somewhat rigid—don't you think?" But before Jim could muster an answer, she pushed him even harder. "I'd think a chaplain would consider the needs of the patient, first, and not get all hung up on theological or sacramental distinctions. It seems to me such distinctions are important, but not vital, when it comes to bringing comfort to a dying soul who is obviously a Christian brother or sister. I doubt very much that dying patients are interested in sacramental distinctions of that kind. My Theo always asserted that one needs to be extremely careful not to confuse the 'traditions of men' and the 'desires of God' for his children in need."

Without hesitation Jim retorted, "Well, I don't agree."

Getting to his feet he walked over to the small window separating the lounge from the busy hallway. Turning back to her, he continued, "Maybe the distinctions were man-made but they were inspired by God. That's the whole point of honoring the Catholic Tradition. It's not merely a human fabrication. Our Tradition has been inspired by God, our Magisterium is guided by the Holy Spirit, and our pontiff is the 'vicar of Christ' on earth. I think that being 'rigid' is a viable alternative to being 'confused' or compromised."

Doris knew only too well that this conversation was not going to advance beyond the entrenched position her newest dialogical partner had taken, so she ended it, saying, "Let's pray that you never have to make that choice, as it could prove very painful and difficult."

Returning to his place on the couch, Jim agreed, "Right you are, enough of that!"

The music was interrupted by an announcement. "Father Jim O'Connor. Chaplain O'Connor. Please dial 4676."

Jim jumped to his feet. "That's for me; I'd better see what it's all about. Please, excuse me."

After placing the call and finding that there was no emergency, Jim returned to find Doris still sitting on the couch. She jumped to her feet as he reentered the room. "I'm sorry, Father, I had no way of knowing. I'm accustomed to clergy in clerical dress and . . . ."

Before she could finish her thought Jim reassured her, "It's my day off."

Without giving it a thought Doris inquired, "Do you know my husband? Have you met Theo?"

Jim cast his eyes to the worn carpet of the lounge. "Yes, I've met him. His roommate was one of my parishioners—Mr. Wagner?"

Doris' eyes filled with tears. "Would you be so kind as to stop in to visit my husband, I know he'd love to speak with you."

Standing up and stepping toward the entrance to the lounge Jim assured her, "Of course I'll visit. And thank you once more for sharing this thoughtful conversation with me."

Later that night, long after visiting hours had ended, Theo lay in his bed close to sleep. It had been a day, heavy with pain and great discomfort of soul for Theo. Doris had told him about Jim O'Connor and their conversation and that he'd promised to visit.

Sitting at his desk in the chaplain's office Jim was thinking about Doris and their conversation. Had the question about the sacrament and a "dying patient" actually been accidental—pure chance—or was it providential? Was he being challenged, as he'd been so often in his youthful ministry, to grow, to stretch, to see God's hand in the most unexpected of places? God's Spirit moved throughout human encounters. Was his encounter with Doris Cross one such meeting? Had he been unable to see 'the forest for the trees," being more "rigid" than he should in this ministry of chaplaincy? Jim prayed for divine wisdom, for guidance, for Christ-like compassion.

As Theo began to drift off into sleep, as he began to cross over that boundary between the real world and his world of dream-drama, a hand touched his shoulder ever so softly. Theo opened his eyes.

Standing by his bed was Jim O'Connor, holding a chalice in one hand and a white communion host in the other.

"Take and eat," Jim whispered close to Theo's ear; "Take and eat, Theo Cross, this is the body of Christ broken for you—broken for you."

That night Theo slept more soundly than he had in months—no pain, no aching dreams, no lingering longings—just a peaceful, deep sleep. That night Chaplain Jim O'Connor learned that God's *grace* exceeds all boundaries, embraces all souls, enlarges all hearts.

6

Chosen

You did not choose Me, but I chose you. I appointed you that you should go out and produce fruit and that your fruit should remain, so that whatever you ask the Father in My name, He will give you. This is what I command you: Love one another.

JOHN 15:16–17

THE WINTER SUN BROKE through thick clouds, with golden rays piercing the large windowpane, bathing Theo in their warmth. It had been cold and cloudy for several days, with only a peak of sunlight from time to time. Theo lay there, pulling his body into a fetal position, his face to the windowpane, so that the warm glow would cover every part of his being like a blanket.

Theo had always enjoyed the sunshine—even more than snow, hills, and sledding. He would take his grandson on all day fishing excursions to the local lake, spending hours beneath a large oak tree—his favorite spot. With the warm rays touching his face, Theo now shielded his eyes from the blinding light. The patches of blue sky reminded him of the water at the lake—blue, clear, deep, cold. His grandson would always point to the small sunfish at the shoreline, just beneath the surface of the water; his entire day was devoted to "catching those little fishes." When he caught one, he'd fling the fish at Theo demanding he remove it from the hook. It was a game they played, more than it was any apprehension about touching the fish.

It's simply amazing how clearly one remembers those small portraits of life when death is so close at hand. The images, words, smiles, tears, laughter, all appear before the mind's eye as if they are being enacted on a stage—somewhat like a dream-drama. Smells, sights, and sounds are given a life of their own, coming to life again and again—in memory, crystal clear memory. The things once considered of grave importance grow pale before the beauty of fond memories. The small things, those encounters that once seemed insignificant, loom larger than life once overshadowed by the reality of death. Simple things: a walk through a park, a picnic on a lazy summer afternoon, the embrace of a child, a drive in the country, the frantic effort to devour an ice cream cone melting in the warmth of the sun, flowers in bloom, bird song, the chance meeting with a stranger, the scent of an infant or a lover. All these, and more, become the focus of memory when life is overshadowed by the pall of death.

Quite suddenly Theo's mind focused on the thought "strangers," in particular, the young priest, with his gracious provision of Eucharistic joy. As the sunlight showered Theo's body with warmth, so the generous act of the priest had showered the soul of this dying man with "amazing grace."

One memory can unexpectedly give birth to another and another in a string of related events. As the memory of the priest faded, Theo recalled a time in his own life—a time that now seemed so distant it could've been the memory of another—a time when he awakened to a strange tug at his heart and soul. Advancing like soldiers along a frontline, the memories kept presenting themselves to Theo in developing formation—the pieces of a puzzle coming together to form the whole of an image—a memory that made Theo smile.

At the age of fourteen Theo sought the counsel of the parish priest, a young man who had only recently come to the parish from seminary. Theo shared a series of unsettling feelings and thoughts he'd been experiencing for months. He was certain that God had something to do with it, even though he couldn't offer specifics as to why he believed that to be the case. Father McCloud seemed unimpressed and not at all enthused by this "startling news." As if to toss cold water on a heated pubescent boy, he suggested that Theo be patient and wait for further confirmation. "After all," he told Theo, "you are far too young and need to experience more of life before you make such a commitment of your life."

Telling a fourteen year old to be patient is like telling an ant to carry an elephant—the impossibility of the request is simply outrageous! At the age of fourteen, Theo Cross had already been patient, and he wanted answers and action. Not to be dissuaded, Theo sought the support of his parents. To his dismay they shared Father McCloud's dismissive attitude, assuring Theo that he'd change his mind after the first encounter with a female in the back seat of a car. It was crass, but it made the point succinctly enough!

Theo's mother advised him, "You're just a boy for heaven's sake. What do you know about life? Becoming a priest means giving the whole of your life to the Church— and you can't even give your undivided attention to your math homework! Think about it: no cars, girls, dances, or dates. It might be best for you to finish high school before you set your sights on a ten-to-twelve year educational commitment."

His father, on the other hand, simply shrugged his shoulders, took out another cigarette from his breast pocket, and while lighting it concurred, "Well son, you're just a kid! It's just not sane for a kid to make an adult decision. And I've noticed how you gravitate to your uncle's adventure magazines; don't tell me you're reading the stories—I know better! Why not take time—finish high school—and then, we'll see."

Theo persisted. He hounded his parents. He even sought the aid of his grandmother who'd already written to the family in Ireland to inform them that there'd one day be a priest in the family—knowing her support, at least, was assured! On a number of occasions Theo begged his grandmother to raise the subject with his parents, but even she seemed to drag her feet. Theo felt no one was taking him seriously—with the exception of God, who appeared to have his own agenda and was pursuing it like a female lion hunting in the bush.

Then one night at dinner, his grandmother told his parents that Theo had a calling from God to become a priest, and if they stood in His way, the Lord would make their lives a living hell until they came to their senses. It was far more than Theo had expected—or even wanted—but it did the trick. Guilt and fear have a way of making people do the strangest things.

Almost immediately, Theo's parents made an appointment to speak with Father McCloud in order to request that he set up an interview with the seminary admissions team. Father McCloud was reticent to comply with their request, but when Theo's dad showed up at the rectory one evening to make his "strong" feelings known, Father McCloud relented and made the appointment.

A week prior to the Saturday morning when Theo and his parents were to meet with the admissions team, Father McCloud invited them to visit the rectory study for a word of pastoral guidance. His singular word to Theo remained with him for the rest of his life: "Remember," he'd said while puffing on his pipe, "God isn't bound by the strictures of our time. He may well be calling you to this priesthood, but never allow impatience to influence your response. God will work out His will for your life in His own time, His own way, and to His own ends."

Saturday morning finally arrived for Theo. His mom had pressed his best suit and shirt and had hung both on the door to his room. After a light breakfast and politely listening to his grandmother's long, rambling prayer for protection and guidance, father, mother, and son began their journey with an "Irish" blessing. During the length of the trip into the city, with the exception of small talk about the weather or scenery, they remained silent. Finally they arrived at the open gate to the seminary.

The seminary boasted of one-hundred-forty acres of landscaped grounds, with gardens placed strategically for private meditation and prayer. An iron fence which ran the entire length of the perimeter of the property, was extremely ornate, adorned with floral patterns and an occasional relief depicting some scene from the Old or New Testament.

As his father turned the car into the main entrance, Theo held his breath. He'd never been to the seminary and the beauty of it all was breathtaking. He pointed to the huge marble pillars with all the excitement of a child on seeing an amusement park for the first time. "Look at this place," he shouted, "Would you just look at this place!"

Turning and facing Theo with an expression of annoyance, his mom hollered, "For the love of God, Theo, that's my ear you just shouted into! I know you're excited, but you'd better calm down or the priests will think you're a maniac!"

Theo's father stopped to ask a young seminarian in a long cassock if he could please direct them to the central building for admissions. Having found his way, he parked in the section set apart for guests.

Turning to Theo with brush in hand his mother said, "Come here Theo, your hair's a mess! I won't have you going in looking like that."

She thrust the hard bristles of the brush into his thick curls, causing Theo to yell again, only this time in pain, "Ouch!"

Everything in its proper order, Theo, his mother and father made their way to the main building. The entrance was marble with an impressive mosaic of St. Francis in the floor below their feet. Theo whispered to his mom, "Are you sure it's ok to walk on a saint?"

His father glared at him and Theo shot back, "What? I'm not kidding—it's ok, right?"

No answer, and yet another glare of disapproval was his answer.

Larger-than-life oil paintings, taller than Theo's father, were hanging randomly on opposing walls; each depicted a biblical event: the crossing of the Red Sea, Moses on Mt. Sinai, the Visitation to the Virgin Mary, the Crucifixion of Christ, and of course, the Resurrection. It was a dramatic introduction to a life that seemed foreign to anything and everything Theo had ever known, and he wondered what it would be like to be surrounded by so much beauty each and every day.

It was obvious to Theo that silence was strictly enforced on the seminarians and postulates during the chosen hours for prayer and reflection. Numerous as they were—all were silent, walking about, but without a word spoken in the passing. Theo even wondered if he and his parents were invisible to these young men. The trio made their way to the admissions office.

A large ornately decorated door opened at the far end of a long hallway. An elderly priest made his way in the direction of Theo and his parents. Greeting them in the proper order—father *then* mother—with a strained smile, the priest extended his right hand to Theo's parents—father *then* mother—saying, "Welcome to St. Francis Seminary; you must be the Cross family—and this young man must be Theo."

Theo extended his hand and just as quickly withdrew the offer, thinking it a brazen and far too familiar thing to do. "Yes, Father," he replied, "Are we late?" Theo knew his father had allowed ample time for travel and they were, in fact, early for their scheduled appointment—yet the question seemed to him the polite thing to ask.

"No, not at all," said the priest, motioning the three of them to a small waiting room off to the right. "You're not late at all. Can I, perhaps, get you some refreshment while you wait for your scheduled interview. Perhaps some coffee or tea?"

Each declined the gracious offer. The priest invited the family to relax on one of several blush chairs or couches, explaining, "We have two other candidates to interview before your son—before Theo—so please wait here and we'll be with you as soon as possible." Directing them to the nearest restrooms—should they have need—the priest existed the room.

It was only then that Theo noticed the two other young men seated in the waiting room, each with his head buried in a magazine. The elderly priest again appeared at the entrance to the room and extended an invitation to one of the young men to join him in "attending" to his interview.

Theo watched the young man as he walked from the room with his hands held behind his back. He was tall, with blond hair and fair complexion. His eyes were a penetrating blue and were framed by wire-rimmed glasses. Theo judged him to be much older than himself and he looked to be extremely intelligent and serious—perhaps too serious. Theo's attention then focused on the other young man, who by then had dropped the magazine and was simply gazing into space, as if daydreaming. After receiving his parent's permission, Theo approached him, asking, "Do you want to become a priest too?" Theo immediately regretted his action. What a stupid question, he thought to himself, "why else would the guy be seated in the waiting room of an admissions building in a seminary."

"I'd like very much to enter the priesthood. And you?"

Looking over his shoulder at his parents who were whispering while pointing to one of the portraits hanging on a wall, "Well, I think God's calling me to become a priest—but I guess they'll tell me today whether that's true, or just some strange thought in my head."

Removing his glasses and cleaning them with a white handkerchief he pulled from the breast pocket of his blazer, the young man introduced himself. "My name is William Harrison. And you?"

Moving closer, Theo offered, "I'm Theo—Theo Cross—and they're my folks."

Placing the glasses back on his face, the young man replied "It's a pleasure to meet you Theo. How old are you, if you don't mind my asking?"

In a soft, barely audible voice, Theo admitted, "I'll be fifteen in a month."

Harrison stood and approached Theo. "Excuse me, did you say 'fifteen' in a month?"

Theo felt a twinge of anxiety, and quickly added, "But, I don't think age is an issue with God, do you?"

Adjusting the fountain pen in his inner pocket, Harrison said, "No, I guess not. But are you certain you know what you're committing to here? I mean, don't you think it would be better for you to wait until you've had some experience with life."

Feeling a flush of anger on his cheeks, Theo burst forth, "'Experience!' I've had 'experience!' And I'm not sure what that has to do with God's calling me. If God wanted me to have 'experience,' wouldn't he have said so? Like, Ok, I want you to become a priest, but first get plenty of experience."

Theo's voice had risen to such a volume, even his parents were diverted from their conversation and motioned for him to come back and sit with them on the couch. He turned on his heels and walked away from William Harrison, leaving the young man baffled by this nearly fifteen year-old-candidate-for-the-priesthood.

Theo could not understand why everyone—excepting his grandmother and God—thought it best for him to wait and experience more of life before entering seminary. He reasoned that he had to attend school anyway, so why not seminary? Why not now rather than later? But what really baffled him was how no one ever defined exactly what they meant by use of "experience." Wasn't life itself "experience?" Hadn't he, his brothers, and his friends had plenty of "experience?" Wouldn't the death of his brother qualify as "experience?" The word had never once been part of the prayers he prayed or spoken by the tiny voice he'd heard in his head—the small voice he knew to be God's own.

No sooner had Theo completed his train of thought than the elderly priest once again appeared at the entrance to the waiting room. "Mr. Harrison," he said with a smile, "we are ready for your interview. Please, follow me."

On taking his leave William Harrison wished Theo "good luck."

As Harrison disappeared down the hallway, Theo thought, "Now 'luck' has something to do with this whole God-call thing?"

For an hour or more Theo paced back and forth in front of his parents until his father could take no more and reaching out, took Theo by the wrist and pulled him onto the couch beside him, "For the love of God, Theo, just sit here and relax! You're driving me nuts with your nervous energy. All of your pacing like a caged cat isn't going to make the interview come any sooner."

Once more the elderly priest appeared at the entrance to the waiting room. "Theo Cross, we're ready for you now." Looking at Theo's parents the priest added, "I promise you, he won't be long at all!" He then made a motion with his hand that Theo should follow him to the room behind the ornately carved doors.

Upon entering the room behind the elderly priest, Theo's eyes fell on two other priests seated at a large table, papers piled high on the right hand side. Both priests were writing something and hadn't noticed Theo enter the room. When they finally did look up, the older of the two, with hair as white as the walls, slowly stood on his feet and motioned for Theo to sit in a large leather chair directly in front of the table.

Without any formal introductions, they began their questioning of Theo Cross. First one, then the other, then the other—like machines operating in syncopation. "Are you fully aware of the sacrifices you'll be required to make in pursuing this 'calling?'" "Have you discussed this 'call' with your parish priest?" "How do your parents feel about your being here today? What do they make of your 'call?'" "How familiar are you with the life-style of the priesthood?"

"Why are you certain that God has issued this 'call' to the priesthood?" On and on and on they asked question after question, until Theo felt his head spinning.

Theo answered every question to very best of his ability; but it was obvious to him that his answers hadn't impressed his questioners. The interview concluded almost as abruptly as it had begun, and within a matters of minutes, Theo and his parents were sent on their way with one simple piece of advice: "Theo, we think it best that you finish high school, perhaps junior college, get some life-experience, and then return for another interview. We'll hold on to your file and pray for you to receive clear, unambiguous direction from God regarding your 'call' to the priesthood. If the 'call' is genuine, God will continue to open doors and direct your life accordingly. If not, it's best that you find out before committing to seminary education and years of study, disciplined prayer and meditation."

As Theo and his parents emerged from the admissions building, and while passing through those massive marble pillars, Theo Cross felt a sense of relief. Even though he wasn't quite certain why, it felt ok. He was relieved that the interview was now over; relieved that there were no more questions to dodge or answer; relieved that he could go to the dance next weekend; relieved that he could again think about the car he hoped to own one day; relieved that he could continue to date his girlfriend; relieved that perhaps he'd been wrong about the 'call' to the priesthood after all.

Stepping beyond the pillars, Theo watched as the courtyard just beyond filled with seminarians—some laughing, others deep in discussion; this was a time between the hours for prayer and thoughtful reflection—a time for companionship. Across the courtyard stood a statue of St. Francis, clad in a flowing cloak, his right arm extended, his finger pointing to the world beyond the fence surrounding the seminary campus. The small smile breaking the corners of the mouth of St. Francis, reminded him of the statue of Mary in the cemetery where his brother slept in death.

Theo thought about his brother and life experience and the need to wait for God to finalize the 'call' to—what? Then a thought: "You'll answer, but it'll not be here." As if in answer to his question, Theo heard a voice assuring him, "But you'll one day answer with joy."

Taking one last, long look at the beauty surrounding him, Theo put his arms around his mom and dad and said, "Let's go home."

7

The Never Forgotten

Now faith is the reality of what is hoped for, the proof of what is not seen. For our ancestors won God's approval by it.

HEBREWS 11:1–2

"MR. CROSS," SPOKE THE nurse standing at Theo's bedside, "I'm going to close the curtain.

You're getting a new roommate. Perhaps you can get acquainted once he's settled in. I hear you have a gift for making new friends." With that, she pulled the curtain, concealing the other bed, but also blocking Theo's view of the hallway; thus he found himself gazing out the window at the canopy of a deep blue sky and bright sunlight bathing the city below. Theo's mind wandered back to his trip to St. Francis and the long road that awaited him in seeking God's clarity on the "call"—the call that caused him to make the seismic shift from Roman Catholicism to Reformed Presbyterian. He thought about the mystery of pastoral ministry, and about his call to serve at First Presbyterian in the heart of the city and at the age of thirty-six. He thought about the mystery of pastoral ministry. Finally, Theo Cross murmured a prayer beneath his breath: "*Holy Spirit, you work in mysterious ways, your wonders to perform.*"

The new patient's name was Mark Johnston, a man about thirty-six years of age, with wild hair and correspondingly intensely curious eyes, eyes that looked beneath and within. Theo observed that Johnston's eyes blazed with curiosity and that his laughter broke free from his face like thunder. Johnston was nothing like Theo's former roommate, the late Mr. Wagner, and Theo was curious to see just how different they were. Theo soon discovered that Johnston was not one to keep his thoughts to himself, and apparently had no qualms about crossing over personal boundaries and invading the privacy of others. In the course of their first conversation, Theo learned more about Mark Johnston than he'd learned about Wagner in the entire time they'd been roommates.

"Dr. Johnston," as he preferred to be called, was a professor of philosophy at one of the local universities. He'd studied at Yale and was chosen to be a Rhoads Scholar at Oxford University. His accomplishments were impressive, including several ground breaking books in Metaphysics and Existentialism. He was married, with four children ranging in ages from three to ten years. He and his wife had met while studying at Yale, and she practiced law at one of the most prestigious firms in the city. Mark Johnston had been admitted to the hospital after a severe case of intestinal flu, which his doctor felt needed further care, as he had experienced several occasions when he had serious passing of blood.

It was during their second evening as roommates that Dr. Johnston and the Rev. Dr. Theo Cross would "lock horns." After the evening meal had been cleared away, Mark Johnston drew-up a chair beside Theo's bed and asked a question that provoked immediate reaction, like a match head igniting on dry grass: "How long have you been a Christian?"

Dreading the possibility that this was a prelude to one of those pointless philosophical debates, Theo answered, more out of politeness, than any other motive, "All my life. Why do you ask?"

Mark pulled at the bed sheet as if contemplating the next strategic move, "Just curious I guess; wondering to myself if you give a great deal of thought—you know, time and energy—to thinking about God." He then leaned over the bedrail, placing his chin on his hands—like a child about to ask a probing question of his attentive parent—"I would *think* someone in your profession is always *thinking* about God in some fashion or another."

"Well, yes," replied Theo, pausing to adjust his bed sheets, "I suppose you could say that I spend a great deal of time thinking about God. Yet I think it's far more important that I have faith in God, and that I focus on the relational aspect of our communion, living my life as best I can in light of what I understand to be God's will for my life—making daily choices according to what I believe is God's will."

Mark's intensely curious eyes opened wide, "God's will? And just *how* can *you* ever be certain that *you* know *God's* will?"

The emphases on certain words was not lost on Theo. "As a Christian, I believe God's will has been revealed in the witness of the Scriptures and ultimately in Jesus Christ as God's Word incarnate."

Mark's face broke into a small, somewhat cynical smile. Yet Theo continued, "I simply can't think about God without also, at the same time, thinking about myself: how I live my life, the way I treat other people, the choices I make each and every day—for good or for evil."

Leaning back in his chair Johnston announced, "You're a good *existentialist* Theo Cross!"

Theo propped himself up on his elbows. "Okay, if you feel the need to pigeon hole me, than I suppose I'm a good 'existentialist,' as you say. But I've never thought the Christian faith was anything other than existential, if by that you mean having to do with existence in every aspect and in all its fullness."

The response didn't seem to affect Johnston one way or the other; he simply leaned forward and said, "Well, that's a terribly simplistic definition, but I understand what you're driving at, I suppose." Then after glancing out the window at the panorama of the city, Johnston began to ask a serious of rapid fire questions—questions that awakened in Theo a genuine concern for the welfare of Mark's soul: "How do you feel about death and dying? I mean do you ever concern yourself with death and what's beyond? What if all these years you've been mistaken—death is death, nothing more and nothing less" What if, perchance, your 'beliefs' haven been misguided—even mistaken—false and misleading? What then?"

It certainly wasn't the first time Theo had faced the same or similar questions, but coming from Mark Johnston the questions felt to Theo more like a test or a challenge.

Taking a drink from his Styrofoam cup, Theo replied, "First of all, it wouldn't be as disturbing as your questions imply—only because faith isn't a matter of cerebral certitude or rational confirmation of some proposed facts. The difficulty I have with your questions is their presupposition or basis. Should this belief system all prove to be a falsehood, then God is, *de facto*, the 'father of lies.' That would make God, *de jure*, a manipulative, cruel, and ugly deity! So, is God a liar, Mark? Is God ugly? Is God cruel?"

Brushing his hand through his thick hair, Johnston admitted, "I haven't a clue! Maybe the God of Christian belief is no more than a projection of human need and aspiration, projected or written large on the face of the universe. Perhaps no such God, or no god, exists at all—you know, the God of mercy, love, and forgiveness, not to mention 'eternal life.' God could be one huge fabrication of human imagination, evolving over the centuries, out of a deep need for meaning or purpose, or the desire for a larger reality than this life. You know as well as I do that this life can be absurd, pointless, depressing in the face of inevitable death."

Theo began to feel empathy for this young philosopher, who seemed to have taken the best insights of philosophical conviction and used them as fodder for the creation of his own belief system, one that originated in a failing sense of life as purposeful and in many ways quite beautiful. He remembered an incident from a story in the *Book of Acts*, in which the Apostle Paul was accused of having his "great learning" cause him to go "mad." When applied to Mark Johnston, it wasn't to be cruel—simply honest.

Assuming a tone more personal, less academic, Theo explained, "Mark, I'm really in no mood to argue about the existence of God from a philosophical point of view! But I'll gladly tell you what I hold as a deep and deliberate conviction. Being Christian means, at least in part, thinking about the inevitability of death long before one draws that final breath. Death can come to any person, long before he or she takes the labored breath of death itself. You can die to all that's rich, good, and exciting in life; you can die to the wonderful, joyous, invigorating opportunities in life, long before the doctors pronounce a fatal prognosis! You can choose 'death' as a way-of-life-and-living, becoming dead to hope, dreams, and expectations. Then you become 'dead' even in the presence of, what by faith I call, the living

God who confers all life. I've witnessed far too many souls who've become 'dead' in heart, soul, mind, and spirit—long before the physical termination of their life."

With a look of both astonishment and anger, Johnston jumped to his feet, "For Christ's sake, Cross, I was just asking about your thoughts on God and not begging for some watered down philosophical perspective on being 'dead' even—as you say—'before taking that final breath!' I make it my business to think about God and it hasn't made any difference in my life at all. I've never once thought myself 'dead' in heart, mind, or soul—whatever the hell they are, or whatever you make of them. My interest is solely in the intellectual fabrication of a concept of a transcendent being—whatever *you* wish to call it—simply because of the interest it holds for me, an exercise in intellectual exploration into the human need for transcendence; and here you come on with a sermon of some kind!"

Theo pressed his head into his pillow, his eyes still fixed on Mark's face, and responded, a bit tongue-in-cheek, "No, not a sermon! If it'd been a sermon, it would've been better prepared!"

Johnston sat down, a smile braking out over his face.

Silence filled the space between them. After a long moment, Theo continued, "Mark, I don't have all the answers to all the questions—then again, does anyone? I certainly don't have the complexities of human life all figured out, and I struggle with questions of life and death each and every day of my life. Now, I face my own death. For God's sake, man, do you think I—or any Christian—anticipates, really anticipates death with glee and excitement? What choice do we have, any of us, but to face the inevitability of death with integrity and grace? I don't have a choice in death; I do have a choice as to whether I face death with fear or faith, with hope or despair, with grasping or with graceful release of this life."

Mark again leaned on his elbows, deep in reflective consideration of this elderly man's honesty.

With his voice almost gone, Theo conceded, "Maybe we Christians do give others the impression that for us life isn't terribly complex and the answers are always easy to find in our Bible or faith traditions. Yet any Christian disciple, worthy of the title, knows that just isn't the case. Like everyone else, we Christians must make a choice each day to take life by the throat, so to speak, to live fully and freely in light of all the richness of life's paradox and perplexity. The rest is—as we say—in the hands of God and His *grace*."

———————◇———————

As the evening sun began to cast a dark crimson flame across the skyline above the city in the distance, Mark lifted his head and gazed out the window. It was a compelling and beautiful sight to behold, a city bathed in a light that, while fading, still had the power to illuminate with great charm. It was enough to make a person feel overjoyed to be alive. Seldom had Mark felt that way about anything, as his life was consumed with research and writing. Whereas he once took long walks with his wife and children, now he spent long hours over the lap top and with yet another manuscript-in-the-making. Now, somehow, *Nihilism and the Doctrine of Creation* did not seem all that profound a contribution to scholarship. In the presence of this beauty and wonder, Mark thought it possible that even *he* could believe in a God of creation whose beauty was conferred on a cosmic realm of existence. Suddenly Mark's thought turned to his wife, his children, and life in general—the purpose and meaning of it all.

Theo had left Mark to his private thoughts. Once having regained his attention, Theo continued his sharing, "What I was saying was that there seems to me only one choice facing each of us in this life; one that confronted everyone from Moses and his people to Jesus and his disciples—and that's whether we'll choose to live as though we were 'dead' to God, God's will and purpose for our lives, or choose to live life in the light of God and His love—with hope, promise, and joy; with mercy, love, and respect for the integrity of every human life."

Theo suddenly also noticed the vibrant colors breaking over the city skyline. "Life! That's what God is all about Mark—life! With all of its ambiguity and frustration, all of its surprises and expectations, all of its failures and triumphs; it's life—not death! God desires life. God *is* life and more. But at the very least—life! There's a passage in the Bible that reads: 'God is not the God of the dead, but of the living.' That's intended to mean even those who've died are held in some form of life before God. It's a mystery well beyond the capacity of our tiny human intellect to comprehend!"

One of the nurses entered the room to caution Theo to lower the volume; his voice could be heard as far as the nurse's station! Mark stepped in to defend Theo, saying, "He's fine, nurse, just a little excited, that's all! Seems I aroused a sermon in Pastor Cross. I hope you won't deny a 'dying man' a taste of excitement in life!" The nurse however was unimpressed with Mark's commentary and simply told them to maintain a respectful level of voice as, "There are other patients on this floor besides the two of you!"

After she'd left the room, Theo motioned to have Mark sit on the edge of his bed, like an invitation he'd have given his daughter Jessica. Once Mark was seated, Theo picked-up the conversation again. "Dr. Johnston, as a professor of philosophy you can't be surprised at what I'm sharing, as if it were original with me! But for the sake of our keeping company, what if we *could* choose to live life as though 'dead' to God—coming from nowhere and going nowhere, as though life were meaningless, an absurdity, a cruel drama without plot, purpose, or resolution? Isn't it possible that we'd then become so disillusioned with life, we'd become 'dead' to every single aspect of human existence—even the most powerful and profound? And I mean 'dead' to the possible, to changes we could otherwise envision enlarging our relationship with family and friends; 'dead' to the promises of today's differences and tomorrow's new day; 'dead' to the promise that our bitterness of today could find healing in a new tomorrow of forgiveness and *grace*? 'Dead' Mark—we can be as 'dead' in life as we will be inevitably beneath that definitive pall!"

Theo literally collapsed in utter exhaustion, sinking deep into his pillow, now saturated with sweat. It was so unlike him to get that excited about anything. He dried his brow with a washcloth from his bed stand, then held the cloth over his face to conceal the tears forming in his eyes. While it was fine for Mark to see Theo excited, his tears were another matter altogether! What Theo feared most wasn't Mark's rejection or ridicule of his tears, but that the mere sight of them would cause Mark to perceive what Theo had shared was merely the babbling of a Christian sentimentalist.

But in fact, Mark's reaction was completely unexpected, even to him, as he was developing a deep respect for this man who'd expended so much energy from an already enfeebled frame, trying to make his faith clear to another. Actually, it was far more than that! Here was a mere shadow of a man, his body wasting away from this dread disease, thundering his faith of hope in the ears of someone who could (and would) walk away from this hospital to "get on with the living of his life."

Mark looked at Theo, washcloth still pressed to his face, wondering how long he would live: another week, another day, perhaps no more than an hour. Once again, Mark's thoughts turned to his wife and children. He tried to imagine *himself* in the place of Pastor Theo Cross.

Professor Mark Johnston had never considered himself a "bad" person. He'd never hurt another person intentionally; he'd never given even a thought to robbing a bank, taking drugs, or beating his wife and children. After all, he was "good enough" to "think" about God—which was more than many others could claim. He'd always donated generously to local community service organizations and charities. He was even active in a local soup kitchen and homeless shelter. No, Mark Johnston wasn't a "bad" person at all. And yet, for all that—there was still something lacking, a void in his life. He'd never before thought about a choice between a "way of life" or a "way of death" as a daily reality of human existence. He couldn't help but wonder if, perhaps, he hadn't been one of those "walking dead" alluded to in Theo's observation on life. Could that be the source of his nagging sense of pessimism about almost everything: life, waning friendships, family ties, the meaning and purpose of his life and that of his children—even the universe itself? His wife would often say, in frustration, "You are the most negative soul I know Mark!" Mulling over the words he'd heard fall from the lips of this man, living as he was on the edge of life itself, Mark wondered if maybe he hadn't relegated God to the confines of intellectual curiosity, the ultimate academic conundrum, a compelling issue for philosophical reflection—all in order to keep God at a safe distance. Turning the chair so that he could straddle it like a horse, he faced Theo, and asked, "Pastor, how exactly *do you think* about God?"

After a long, drawn out pause, Theo removed the cloth from his face, revealing his eyes. For the first time Mark saw the dark circles surrounding Theo's gaze—a mark of his physical exhaustion from the interminable battle with cancer. They were like craters on the moon, catching all of the luminosity of this man's valiant struggle with God, life, and death. The wires and tubes protruding from Theo's thinning frame prompted Mark to think he looked like a small sapling, with thin branches and stems reaching out into their room.

Theo had gazed off into the distance, as though he were connecting with another in the unseen distance beyond, then lifting his skeletal hand, he motioned Mark to pull the chair even closer. In a barely audible whisper, he pressed on, even more intently. "I'm losing my voice; you'll have to listen carefully. I'd like to tell you something that was once shared with me by another departing soul. He told me that whenever he thought of God, he thought of God as the seasons of the year—constant, yet changing. Summer, then fall, then winter, then spring; each bringing changes and surprises. You know the changes are coming but they're never the same; year in and year out, you never know in advance what surprises each season will hold."

Mark gazed at Theo with child-like fascination and anticipation, waiting to hear what this dying man was next going to say. As if to answer him, Theo concluded, "Now, that's how I think about God." Then he had another thought. "You know, Mark, when a teacher passes along an insight, some new teaching, some revelation, it quickly becomes the property of the student's heart, soul, and life. That's what this man gave to me. It's in my soul; it's become part of me and the way I think about God."

Another nurse entered the room, distributed the appropriate medication to each patient, and was gone. Theo asked Mark to "refresh" his memory, which thing Mark was glad to do. "You were taking about the teacher and student, and about God as related to the seasons of the year; and, oh, about this as a new thought given you by another."

Theo rolled his eyes. "It's God of course! Always it's God!" Adjusting his position to limit the pain, Theo continued "Whenever I think about God now, I think about him like the changing seasons of the year. He is ever constant in his love, compassion, mercy, forgiveness, grace, and joyful embrace of our lives; yet, He's full of surprises: some exciting, some alarming, some even disturbing. They're strange; a fascinating mixture of the expected and the unanticipated, just like life, Mark. If we choose God and not death, we choose life and love; we choose something greater than despair and dismay; we choose to embrace the mystery, the unanticipated. We choose to anchor our existence in something—some One—other than our self—so that constancy and change become the sum and substance of life's grand journey."

Mark could see that Theo was now completely exhausted, so he stood, moved the chair to the far wall, and observed, "Very interesting, Pastor. Very curious way of thinking about God, I must admit."

Theo asked Mark to draw the curtain around his bed, pleading, "I'm completely played out; I'm going to sleep now. Have a good sleep Mark, and thank you for hearing me out. Who knows?" These were the last words spoken before Theo drifted off, sleeping through the entire night for the first time in weeks.

A gentle nudge awakened Theo from sleep; it was Mark, dressed and apparently ready for discharge. Theo attempted to clear the sleep from his eyes, but the wires and tubes restricted his movement. Mark picked up the wash-cloth and gently wiped Theo's eyes. "I'm going home," Mark told him as he drew the sheets up over Theo. Recalling their conversation, he continued, "Pastor Cross, I wanted to thank you for sharing your faith with me. I've never been very good at this kind of thing, but I wanted to thank you for giving me something to take with me. Can I call it *grace*? Regardless, I think you're right about the 'teacher' and 'student.' But that's not what I wanted to thank you for; I mean, not that one thing. Actually, I want you to know that you're words have touched me. Your image of God is quite beautiful, regardless of where and how you came by it. It's really beautiful." Looking into the eyes of Theo for the last time, Mark concluded, "Pastor, you've obviously made a difference in this world! Philosophers, like me, are a 'dime a dozen.' People like you, people who not only have faith but give others courage, hope, and promise are a rare breed! For what it's worth, I wanted you to know that the next time I teach a course on God and human existence, it will include your observation—your gift of *grace* to me."

Theo motioned for Mark to come even closer to his side. "That's wonderful, Dr. Mark, but please remain open to the possibility that God has a richer and grander pur-pose for your life as well! You're a bright young man; please, never confuse 'faith' in God with 'belief' about God. It's 'faith' that makes all the difference—'faith' professor, like a child's faith in the parent, like a spouse's faith in the spouse, like life itself."

Picking up his suitcase, Mark assured him, "I won't forget. I'll never forget you, Pastor Cross." Mark Johnston then did something he hadn't done since the death of his own father; he bent over and kissed the forehead of Pastor Theo Cross. Then, he was gone. Once more Theo was alone with his thoughts, his God, his life, and his death.

8

Never Lose Hope

"Listen, Israel: The LORD our God, the LORD is One. Love the LORD your God with all your heart, with all your soul, and with all your strength. These words that I am giving you today are to be in your heart. Repeat them to your children. Talk about them when you sit in your house and when you walk along the road, when you lie down and when you get up. Bind them as a sign on your hand and let them be a symbol on your forehead. Write them on the doorposts of your house and on your gates."

DEUTERONOMY 6:4–9

FOLLOWING HIS EXPERIENCE AT St. Francis Seminary, and with every succeeding year, Theo became more and more disillusioned and dissatisfied with the Roman Catholic Church. He hardly ever attended Mass and never attended to the Confessional. Theo's parents felt that it was just a rebellious stage their son was going through, and his grandmother was certain he would one day return to "the one true Church."

Eventually, Theo became a "problem child" for the nuns in the parochial school, and his parents thought it best to register him in a public school, which Theo attended until graduating from High School. It was during this time that Theo first laid eyes on Doris and fell in love. After graduating from High School, and without prospect of a job, Theo reluctantly followed the counsel of Uncle Dan and entered a local college in the fall, while Doris attended a college in another state.

Theo never returned to the Catholic Church; in fact during the first year of college, Theo separated himself from all things "religious." In exchange, he filled the void with excessive partying and drinking. On one occasion, while driving back to campus from a party, Theo had an accident in which he almost killed a mother and her two small children. Theo spent most of his college nights avoiding his course work and in the local bar; he was adrift, aimless—lost.

This time was filled with anger, bitterness, and resentment; Theo despised all talk about God, and even called Christians silly and stupid. They didn't "get" how bad life could be. Their foolish superstitions weren't going to change that! Theo's parents disapproved of his "new" friends, reminding him on more than several occasions that, even though college students, they were "really bad characters" who would one day "ruin his life—irrevocably."

Then one Easter Sunday morning, alone and walking through a neighborhood close to his campus, Theo found his way into a worship service at a tiny Protestant congregation. Even after all these years Theo still felt a familiar "tug" during the early portions of the service, but decided it was the onion bagel he'd had earlier that morning, or perhaps the coffee. The service was unlike any Theo had ever experienced, with people audibly offering prayers and voices escalating in praise until reaching a pitch that would instill passion in even the most repressed worshipper. Theo didn't sing, didn't join in the responsive readings, and didn't think he'd make it through the entire worship service. But then he heard again *the* voice, the very same voice that had spoken to him as he left St. Francis seminary following his interview: "You'll one day answer with joy."

The pastor was middle aged, a good looking man with fine black hair and a soft, though commanding, voice. When he spoke the congregation sat, spell bound, hanging on his every word. But it was when he read the Scriptures that Theo sat up and took particular notice. The words of Jesus, the images of the surrounding Judean countryside, the voices of the people in distress, the anguished cries of the demons in flight from their human homestead, all came to life in a way Theo had never thought possible. He recalled the voice of the priest droning out the liturgy and readings, always a flat monotone, without feeling or meaning. This pastor, however, brought Scripture to life with heartfelt conviction and a passion unparalleled in the worship experience of Theo Cross.

Even as a child, Theo loved Easter Sunday, with its message of the resurrection and eternal life. After the darkness and dreadful experiences of Holy Week, it was such a relief to hear some "good news." All of that would recede into the background of memory on this particular Easter Sunday morning, replaced by a powerful and life-altering encounter—unexpected and surprising in its spiritual consequence.

Stepping into the elevated pulpit, the pastor stretched out his arms and declared, "This is the eternal symbol of the love of God for us in Jesus Christ—the cruel cross of Calvary!"

Theo held his breath, hoping the pastor would say no more about that "cruel cross." After all, this was Easter; what about the resurrection, the hope, the joy?

As though reading the minds of his congregants, and in particular the morning guest, Theo Cross, the pastor continued with arms outstretched, "We must never allow the joy of Easter Sunday to cause a lapse in our memory! We must not forget the darkness of that place called Golgotha—Place of the Skull! We must never forget how the Risen Christ is the Crucified Christ, bearing the wounds of his saving compassion even into the glory of the heavenly courts. We cannot embrace this morning's message of joy if we forget or forsake the pain of yesterday's dark tomb or Friday's dreadful event or the agony of open wounds inflicted on the body of Him who is Lord of all!"

Theo was fascinated by the pastor's message; the words drew a picture of Golgotha in his mind's eye. Here it was, Easter Sunday, and with the entire congregation, Theo Cross found himself standing at the foot of the cross of Jesus—the Cross of Christ.

The pastor continued to paint a verbal picture of the event, so graphic that Theo almost felt the rain beating on his face and heard the anguished cries of men hanging on the crosses. Swinging his arms as though to embrace the entire congregation, the pastor spoke with deep, sincere emotion: "For you! The Cross of Jesus Christ was for you! For us! The Son of God gave Himself to the agony of this death for us and for our salvation! That cruel cross, that dark instrument of torture, that horrific implement of execution, has become the symbol of God's eternal love and gracious gift of salvation. Embrace the paradox—love taking shape as a crucified Savior; embrace the irony—God's grace disclosed on such an inglorious and brutal instrument of destruction. Death is to be conquered—but the Cross of Christ comes first!"

On occasion one of the congregants would jump to her feet and shout "Amen! Herald that Word to the World! Amen!" Theo had heard about this kind of spontaneous response to preaching, people in the congregation "slain in the Spirit," unable to contain their spiritual enthusiasm. He always thought that such enthusiasm was limited to Pentecostal churches—but before entering worship, Theo was certain this one church was mainline, more traditional in liturgical form; another unexpected, another surprise, another seasonal shift.

After a long and purposeful pause and with his eyes scanning the congregation as though searching for someone in particular, the pastor lifted one of his long fingers and pointed to the cross behind him: "Do you see this object of devotion? We stand beneath this cross and worship the One who died on this cross. And why is that? Why do we worship someone who died like a common criminal? Why do we give our lives to this crucified leader? Why do we place our hope, trust, and faith in a man who was—for all intents and purposes of the time—a failure?"

Theo moved to the edge of the pew, straining to hear the answer; anxious for the answer like a child awaiting the first light of Christmas morning.

"We love this crucified leader because He first loved us! He loved us so much that He went to the cross and with arms outstretched, sucked into His own precious life all the poison of our sinful existence, replacing that same poison with the cleansing waters of His eternal grace, mercy, forgiveness, and salvation. Jesus stretched out His merciful arms, embracing all people in a 'love divine, all loves excelling.' He died for our sins, for my sins, for your sins, for the sins of countless generations, for people everywhere, in every time, beyond time, in every place—all! He gave His body and blood for us—as He shares his divine life with us, with me, with you—His eternal life of love unending."

Theo fell back in the pew with a sense of relief, telling himself that the pastor's words were not really for him, but intended for someone else, some other member of this congregation—little or none of this message was going to sink beneath the hardened and calloused spiritual skin that had formed and calcified around the aching heart of Theo Cross.

Then it happened! With the speed of a lightning flash, the pastor pointed a finger at Theo—the very same finger that had only moments before pointed to the cross, "You" the pastor said as he locked his eyes on Theo, "Jesus Christ died for you. Not just for humankind in general; not for some generic humanity—for you, sir, for you! Your sins are written in blood and in bold letters upon the Cross of Christ. Did you actually think He'd forget you? Did you honestly believe He was no longer concerned with the state and value of you as a soul? Do you think He'll ever permit one of His lost sheep to remain out there in the wilds, without comfort, or security, or the peace of His eternal love? Have you truly convinced yourself that He'd turned His back on your life, as it descended into the hell of life's turmoil, tragedy, and disgraceful existence? Those nail scarred, resplendent hands are reaching for you, sir—for you—here, now, this moment. He's calling you home—finally, forever—home! If He didn't die for *you*, then He didn't die for any of us."

Again, Theo heard *the* voice: "You'll one day answer with joy!"

Anyone who has been in the church for a number of years, and has experienced the movement of the Holy Spirit, will testify to the way in which such an experience of God's grace can be and often is overwhelming, as one is literally compelled to obedience. The Holy Spirit comes upon one like a holy fire, a brilliant light illuminating all that is within one's heart, soul, mind, and spirit. It isn't a burden *at all* to comply with the guidance of the Spirit; one doesn't feel a loss of personal freedom, but the enlargement of one's freedom. The presence of the Holy Spirit gives birth to an unspeakable joy, encompassing the whole of one's being. During the proclamation of the Gospel the Holy Spirit has been making his presence felt for more than two millennia. In a small sanctuary, on this Easter Sunday, the Holy Spirit moved in such a way, with profound deliberation, bringing this pastor and Theo Cross into the closest communion— an intimate, intentional, grace-full "holy" communion.

Taking a white handkerchief from the pulpit the pastor mopped the sweat from his brow. With the empowerment and insight given him by the Holy Spirit, he focused his gaze on Theo Cross. "Were you there when they crucified my Lord? Were you there, sir, when they stripped Him of His garments and His dignity and nailed Him to the tree? Were you there when the people hurled their curses and abuses at Him, wagging their heads in disgust and shouting all manner of slander? Were you there as the soldiers divided His clothing and gambled them away? Were you, sir? Were you there when they crucified my Lord?"

It was a moment that seemed to Theo an eternity. He held his head in his hands, tears streaming down his face— shame welling up from his soul.

The pastor reached out a hand, as if to comfort Theo: "You were there, weren't you? We've all been there and are there with you even now." Sweeping his hand over the entire congregation, the pastor continued, "We were all there, shouting with the crowd, hurling our abuses, watching in shame from afar. He saw you, us, each and all of us. And what did He say? Did He swear that He'd one day get His revenge? Did he tell us that we were all destined for hell in a hand basket?"

Suddenly there was a low, murmuring sound, as the congregation began to hum a tune unfamiliar to Theo, but beautiful in its rhythms. The pastor's voice now took on the resonance of tenderness and affection. "No, my friend; no, my brothers and sisters; what he said was, 'Father, forgive them!' Do you hear His voice; do you hear Him my brothers and sisters? He said, 'Father, forgive them!'"

Once again fixing his gaze on Theo, the pastor spoke softly, saying, "*In this the love of God is made manifest among us: in that, while we were yet sinners, Christ died for us*! For you, son, for me, for us—Christ died for all. There's nothing you can do, nothing I can do, nothing we can do; there's nothing any of us can do that will '*separate us from the love of God in Christ Jesus our Lord.*' That's why we're all gathered here on this Easter Sunday. This crucified One is living among us still—to forgive, to heal, to make us whole, extending grace to us! He's here, even now, with His nail scarred hands touching your broken heart, your soul, and forgiving you your sins—even though they are many. He's here, the Lord of life and death, to forgive us: again, and again, and again—today, tomorrow, and forever. Lift up your head; see and receive the salvation prepared for you from the foundation of the world! Your heart is the tomb on this Easter Sunday, emptied of all sin and filled with the triumphant Presence of the victorious Christ. Grace, all grace, forever grace! Thanks be to God!"

Theo felt a weight lifted from his heart and soul; the darkness of his spirit had been driven away by a blinding light. He threw himself into the Savior's arms, just as he had his uncle's on the day of that fateful "yellow" telegram announcing the death of his brother. Only now, Theo felt he was the one who'd died—or at least some part of him had died away. Something new was coming to life within his heart, soul, and spirit. He felt a joy unlike anything he'd ever known, and a freedom that went beyond any liberty he'd ever experienced. Theo Cross had received his redemption, and his Lord! The cross was his, and now, so was the resurrection. Good Friday and Easter Sunday now held the heart of Theo Cross—and with them came the Christ into his life. Now, finally, at long last, Theo belonged to Jesus Christ—and he was certain Jesus Christ belonged with and within him.

The congregation stood on their feet and joined the pastor in singing "Amazing Grace." With the hymn nearing the final verse, the pastor stepped from the pulpit and moved closer to the Communion Table; lifting both cup and bread he announced: "Come to the Table of Jesus Christ. All things are made ready for you. For this is the body and blood of our Savior, given for you. Receive what you are and praise God for the most precious gift of His Son's Presence in the power of the Holy Spirit."

———————◇———————

"Given for you; given for you," Theo thought as he lay in his hospital bed. He remembered the young priest and the late night Eucharist, like a message of redemption—like the word of *grace* he'd received from that pastor on the day of his commitment to Christ as his Lord, his Savior. Theo would be eternally grateful for both and for all those moments of *grace* with which his life had been showered over the years of discipleship and pastoral ministry. Theo was thinking about life and death, redemption and salvation, cross and resurrection, and about God—again he was thinking about God.

"There you go again, off on a magical mystery tour of the theological imagination! Thinking about God again,

Pastor Cross?" It was Rabbi Allen, one of Theo's best friends and favorite people.

Rabbi Allen and Theo had met at the initial meeting of the "ecumenical study group." The rabbi had helped Theo with the formation of this group and had always been one of the more active participants, willing to serve in any capacity and with immense energy and enthusiasm. The meetings were never without some humorous anecdote, story, or rabbinic parable from Jewish tradition. Rabbi Allen's conversation was laced with the finest wisdom and the funniest jokes! He could make Theo laugh at anything, but best of all he caused Theo to laugh at himself and his overly grave seriousness in thinking about God.

The rabbi pulled up a chair beside Theo's bed. "What will be next?" he said, "Here we have the supreme irony, a Presbyterian pastor in a Roman Catholic hospital, being visited by a rabbi! Now that, Theo Cross, that's what one could call truly 'ecumenical!'" Rabbi Allen took Theo by the hand, "So, how is my favorite Christian friend feeling today?"

Theo whispered, "Not so good. This pain is much worse than I thought possible; I can't even talk very long without having spasms in my chest and stomach. So, try not to make me laugh—not too often or too hard anyway."

With a wry smile the rabbi assured, "Theo, you know what our tradition says: 'Too much laughter can deaden the mind!' Not something we want to happen to you, my friend! Then what? How can a 'dead mind' think about God?"

Theo placed his hand over his mouth and coughed out a laugh, "You're such a blessing! What are you doing here anyway? Don't tell me you've come just to visit this poor, dying, pastoral soul?"

The rabbi took out a prayer shawl from his coat pocket, placed it over his shoulders and said, "Of course, what else? Have you so quickly forgotten the verse from the *Song of Solomon*: 'Love is as strong as death?' Friends love each other, don't they?"

Theo nodded in agreement, "You're my best friend, Rabbi Allen; you're my best friend!" Theo then asked his friend to crank-up the bed in an upright position. Waiting until the rabbi was seated again, Theo took a deep breath, saying, "Tell me a good story. I'm longing to hear a good story."

The rabbi leaned over, placing his chin on his hand, "A good story. What else could a rabbi tell, but a good story? Let me see, what shall I tell you?"

Furrowing his brow in deep thought, Rabbi Allen sat back in his chair, "Ah, yes! That's the one. Listen to this:

> *When a certain rabbi went to Rome, he chanced to find a jeweled bracelet that belonged to the Empress. An official crier went about proclaiming: "Whoever finds the Empress's bracelet within thirty days shall receive a reward; but if it be found upon him after thirty days—his head will be cut-off!" The rabbi returned the bracelet on the thirty-first day. The Empress asked him: "Did you not hear my proclamation?" "Yes" answered the rabbi. "Then why did you not return the jewel within the thirty days?" "In order" said the rabbi "that you should not say that I feared you. I returned it because I fear God." Whereupon the Empress said "Blessed be the God of the Jews!"*

Sadly, Theo had drifted off into a deep sleep almost from the first line of the story. Nudging his friend on the shoulder to awaken him, Rabbi Allen asked, "Did you, perhaps, hear any of it, my friend?"

With a hint of shame in his voice Theo replied "No, I'm sorry. I just seem these days to fall asleep without warning.

It's like I'm exhausted all the time. Can you tell the story again?"

The rabbi took Theo by the hand, "No need my friend. It was about God, and you already think enough about God! Why don't we talk about anything you wish to discuss—other than God."

A good friend is so very important to the health of one's heart and soul: a gift of God's grace, a companion along the rough ways of life's walk, a tireless advocate whenever one's own voice cannot be heard, a person to keep one grounded in the good. Theo wanted to discuss his coming death and Rabbi Allen was his most trusted friend and colleague.

It seemed so formal to many, but Theo had always referred to Rabbi Allen, not by his first or last name, but always by his title "Rabbi." He did so out of a deep respect for the office his friend held in his own faith community, that of teacher. Theo often prayed that Rabbi Allen would only increase in wisdom, since it seemed to Theo so much a part of his dear friend's character.

"Rabbi," Theo spoke quietly, "you and I have been friends for a long time. Can we talk about my coming death? I know it's coming—no secret there—but I've no one I trust more than you to be honest with me.

Getting up from his seat and moving over to another larger and softer chair in the corner close to the head of Theo's bed, with the window now behind him, Rabbi Allen responded, "Ok, Theo, you talk and I'll listen."

Theo turned his eyes to the ceiling above his bed. "Do you see those cracks in the ceiling?"

Rabbi Allen lifted his gaze to the ceiling. "Yes, of course; interesting pattern. But what's the point?"

Theo looked at his dear friend, "Some time ago now they reminded me of my life. I mean they seemed somehow to symbolize my life; or the pathways I've traveled, the places I've been—explored—exploited. Even the people I've come to know and love were somehow woven into the lines of that ceiling. And then I had the strangest thought. I looked at those random cracks and thought they symbolized the life we live in this world—our life before God— random cracks, brokenness, if you will. Isn't that really the strangest thought?"

Returning his gaze to the ceiling; considering the analogy, Rabbi Allen replied, "No my friend, not so strange as it may at first appear. You're thinking about life because you're dying. When we're filled with life, we seldom think of death; but when death is like a pall cast over our living, we can barely consider anything more important than is our coming death! It makes perfect sense for a Christian to be thinking about life and death, almost in the same breath— living in the same small room of the human soul, if you will. After all, that's the whole of it—isn't it? Life, death, life beyond death; they're all essential to your faith confession, aren't they? And 'brokenness' is equally a part of what you Christians are all about—the cross, the body, the bread. You know this, only because you've heard me say it so often. There's a rabbinic saying, that 'the road to the cemetery is paved with suffering.' So, I suppose there are random cracks in every life."

Theo loved this man, honoring both his wisdom and his sense of humor. He always felt that Rabbi Allen had a way of looking through life, as through a window, and seeing deeper realities than most could or *would* chose to see. Then Theo confided, "I'm scared, you see. I'm scared to death that I'll die in a faithless state of my soul!"

The setting sun broke over the rabbi's shoulder casting two shadows in the floor at his feet. "Well, you should be scared! Not of dying in some faithless state of soul. You should be scared of death itself. Only a fool would say that he has no fear of death."

Rabbi Allen turned to gaze out the window and then turned back to his friend. "I recall the story my grandmother told me about an ancient woman who on visiting a cemetery addressed the graves, saying, "How peacefully you sleep, good souls! Still, if you don't mind, I'd rather not join you in such rest!"'

Then turning his gaze to the floor, as if reaching for words, Rabbi Allen concluded, "Would you say she lacked faith only because she saw death for what it is—beneath or behind the façade of 'rest?' Is her fear of death unnatural or uncommon? I doubt it! From where I sit, she was being honest."

Theo suddenly sat upright in the bed. Reaching for the hand of his friend, Theo cried, "I don't want to die. There's so much life I still want to taste, to live. I'm not ready to die. I want to see my grandchildren graduate from high school—maybe live long enough to see them marry. I want to make love to my wife, to smell the cherry blossoms in full bloom, to sit beneath a deep blue sky on a summer day. God, I want to live; I'm not ready, I'm just not ready!"

With that Theo fell back into the bed in complete exhaustion. Rabbi Allen was not one to demonstrate public emotion, but his friend's plea had brought him to the brink of tears. Moving his chair even closer to the bed rail, he laid his hand on the sheets beside Theo's head. "My friend, what are we to do? This death is a terrible tyrant and loathsome villain, without regard for the pain and sorrow inflicted on human hearts and souls. I'm here with you now, and my spirit is with you even when I'm physically absent. Of course you want to live, and we want you to live. But death is no respecter of human wishes and desires; he simply comes and takes at will—without our consent and without concern for the wreckage left behind in his wake. But we can love you to the very end, my friend. We can stay with you until you draw that final breath and never leave you alone in that most difficult hour, as we'll weep bitter tears in your absence. The rabbis say that 'the world weeps when a fruit tree is cut down,' and we will sorrow over the loss of your living with us. Yet the fruit we've tasted from your life will remain."

Theo could feel the tears of the rabbi falling on his forearm—yet not only his forearm, into his heart and soul as well.

"We can cry together, just as we have laughed together," observed the rabbi, while drying the tears from his eyes. "Let's now laugh through our tears, shall we? I'll tell another story."

> *One day Alexander the Great came to the gate of Paradise and knocked, and the guardian angel asked, "Who's there?" "Alexander" was the reply. Which "Alexander" asked the angel. "The 'Alexander' thundered the mighty warrior, Alexander the Great, "the valiant conqueror of kingdoms." "Well, he's not in here" said the angel in a confused voice—"in fact he could never enter these gates, as only the righteous get to enter here!" Alexander than demanded proof that this was the gate to heaven and a fragment of a human skull was tossed at him on which were written the words "Weigh it!" So Alexander took the portion of skull to his wise men, who then placed it on one side of a scale, while Alexander placed gold and silver on the other side. The small fragment of skull outweighed the gold and silver, so that more was added, and then more—all the crown jewels of Alexander's great wealth—and yet, the fragment of skull outweighed it all. Then one of the wise men dropped a few grains of dust on the eye*

> *socket of the skull, and the whole of it ascended into the heavens. Nothing will satisfy until a man's eye is covered with the dust of the grave."*

Rabbi Allen and Theo sat in silence for the longest time; no words spoken; no words were necessary—just hand touching hand and heart open to wounded heart. Suddenly they were both aware of another presence in the room. It was a woman, dressed in Protestant clerical garb. She excused herself and then identified herself as "the hospital chaplain, on duty for the rest of the evening."

Theo introduced himself and then his friend. Immediately Rabbi Allen said to the chaplain, "Shall I share a story with you?"

Somewhat suspicious and more than a little curious, the chaplain said she'd like that, even if she was already late for her rounds.

Rabbis Allen began:

> *It seems there was this novice priest who saw a young man hanging over the ledge of the twenty-first floor of a building. He rushed into the building, took the elevator to the twenty-first floor, exited the elevator, and ran to the room, which was crowded with police and fire fighters. Having encouraged the priest to speak with the young man, he leaned out the widow closest to the young man and said, "Son, you should think what this'll do to your mother and father." The young man screamed, "I've got no mother or father!" "Well then," said the priest, "think about your wife and child." To which the man replied, "I got no wife and child!" Finally, out of sheer desperation, the priest cried-out, "Well then, for the love of God, think of what this will do to the heart of the Blessed Virgin Mary!" And the young man yelled in anger, "Who the hell is she?" And while lighting*

> a cigarette, the priest said, "Jump, you damned
> Protestant heretic—jump!"

While Theo pressed a hand to his stomach to still of pain of laughter, the chaplain observed, politely, "Cute! But I've got a story for you."

Intrigued, Rabbi Allen encouraged, "Please, I'm dying to hear it, as is Theo, I'm sure."

The chaplain sat on one the remaining chairs and recounted:

> *A Baptist minister and a rabbi were attending a*
> *party. The rabbi stood beside a bowl and dipped*
> *his glass deep into the available punch. With that,*
> *the Baptist minister rushed over the bowl, saying,*
> *"Rabbi, please, don't drink that stuff! You know*
> *it's filled with alcohol!" The rabbi lifted the glass*
> *to his face, saying, "And what's the point?" The*
> *Baptist said, "I'd rather commit adultery than put*
> *that devil's brew to my lips!" With that the rabbi*
> *emptied his glass back into the punch bowl, caus-*
> *ing the Baptist to ask in an alarmed voice: "Why*
> *did you do that?" And the rabbi replied, "I didn't*
> *realize we had a choice!"*

Rabbi Allen laughed in a thunderous voice, grabbing Theo by the arm and crying, "Now that's one to remember, Theo!"

Theo was in tears of both joy and pain; it was such a joy to laugh, even through his tears! When he'd laughed himself out, Theo turned to the rabbi and the chaplain, thanking them for both their humor and their support. "I'm very tired," he continued, "but would be most grateful if we could offer prayer together before you leave me for the evening."

The chaplain stood at the right side of Theo's bed, with Rabbi Allen to the left. The three then locked hands, each in turn offering a prayer for Theo, his family, his congregation, and for all who were facing death that night. Theo remembered the first time the "ecumenical study group" engaged in joint prayer; it was such a blessing to hear prayer offered from the hearts of those representing such a variety of faith communities. He'd often thought that the spread of such groups—with prayer, serious engagement in theology, and open conversation—could break down the barriers of prejudice and divisiveness.

Having finished the prayer, the chaplain shook the hand of Rabbi Allen, and then, before leaving the room, told Theo she would be in to see him again the following week. She had no way of knowing that for Pastor Theo Cross the next week would not come—at least in this world!

After the chaplain left the room, Rabbi Allen turned to the window. "She's a nice young woman; a little too rigid for my taste—but nice!" Then he turned to face his friend, with an obvious look of despair in his otherwise bright eyes. "My dearest friend, I think that I shall not see you again in this world. I'm not a person to mince words—you know this. I'll miss your presence in this world—but I'm equally certain that the memory of all that you've been and are will remain with me until that day when I too close my eyes in death. Theo, we've learned from and taught each other so very much: two who think about God—constantly—sharing wisdom and grace! I think perhaps now, I can let you go in death, my beloved friend in Christ—well—your Christ that is!"

A smile broke on the skeletal face of Theo Cross. "Now I leave you in the hands of the Lord God Almighty. Be at peace, my dear friend, and may the angels lead you into paradise!" With that, Rabbi Allen kissed his friend on the forehead, eyes, cheeks, and mouth. Placing his prayer shawl on his shoulders once more, he offered a prayer in Hebrew—and then, removing his shawl, headed for the door. When he reached the doorway, Rabbi Allen suddenly turned and pronounced, "One more thing: 'As long as a man breathes he should not lose hope!"

His dearest friend gone from his life, but never his heart, Theo gazed up at the ceiling, with those cracks running in each and every direction, and prayed beneath his breath: "Hear O Israel; the LORD our God, the LORD is One. And you shall love the LORD your God with all your heart, and with all your soul, and with all your mind, and with all your strength."

Peace came to Theo Cross. He slept.

9

Death as an Open Door

"For I am persuaded that not death or life, angels or rulers, things present or things to come, hostile powers, height or depth, or any created thing will have the power to separate us from the love of God that is in Christ Jesus our Lord."

ROMANS 8:38–39

THURSDAY, FEBRUARY 29TH, THEO Cross had become completely incommunicative; his life was hanging by a single thread of hope, yet slipping away like water through cupped fingers—through the fingers of his wife, Doris, and the family—Theo's friends and congregants. That morning the doctor had informed the family that it was only a matter of hours. Doris waited in Theo's room, thinking about the life they'd shared, about Jessica and the grandchildren, about life and death—and about God. One of the nurses entered the room and drew the curtain around Theo's bed to provide Doris with some privacy. Glancing up at the ceiling for the first time since her initial visit to Theo's room, Doris noted again the random pattern of cracks running each and every direction. She thought about Theo and his ministry, the numerous paths they'd traveled together in their years of marriage, and the many places they'd seen and shared together. Then, she thought again about life and death and God—about hope, faith, and love.

Doris gazed at her husband's body, thin and yet resting peacefully for the first time—in God only knew how long—ever since the diagnosis and initial treatments. Only on occasion would Theo give a sign of consciousness, as he'd whimper some inaudible words. Doris made no effort to retrieve those words once they were lost.

The sky above the city was a deep blue, with small clouds racing across the horizon, like vehicles on a freeway. The air that day was bitter, biting through one's outer garments, into the skin beneath, like icy fingers on a warm back. Doris touched the windowpane with her hand, leaving behind a ghostlike pattern of her palm and fingers, that faded away as quickly as it appeared. Like life, so short, too short, but only in retrospect—only now it seemed so in the face of her coming loss. She leaned over the bedrail and kissed her husband on the lips, and returning to her seat, she wept—silently.

Jessica entered the room; it was her only visit since that day she'd rushed from the room and wept in the hallway. Theo had always enjoyed his daughter's musical talent—her ability to weave melody into the commonalities of life, with medicinal, healing effect. On numerous occasions Jessica had played one or more pieces of sacred music in the worship service, and always to the great delight of her parents and those in the congregation. She placed her guitar case on the floor beside her father's bed, and stood still, contemplating the great change in his appearance—a small measure of the man she'd grown to know and love with such deep affection.

Doris stood and placed her arms around Jessica's shoulders. "Sweetheart, I'm so glad you're here. I know what this means to your father, just knowing you're here with him—with me." They stood wrapped in a long embrace, crying and sharing a shoulder of sympathy and love.

Then, releasing herself from her mother's arms Jessica walked over to her father, leaned over the bedrail, kissed his forehead and whispered, "I'm here now Daddy. I brought you a gift, a gift for your journey. It's something I know you'll love and I want you to take it with you."

Doris had never before seen her daughter express such a deep love for Theo. She thought to herself, "It's never too late to love completely, even if not perfectly!"

Quietly, so as not to disturb the other patients, Jessica removed the guitar from its case and pulling a chair closer to her father's bed; she strummed the strings with her delicate fingers until the melody took shape. Softly she sang:

> "Jesus I live to Thee, the loveliest and best;
> My life in Thee, Thy life in me, in Thy blest love
> I rest.
> Jesus, I die to Thee, whenever death shall come;
> To die in Thee is life to me in my eternal home.
> Whether to live or die, I know not which is best;
> To live to Thee is bliss to me, to die is endless rest.
> Living or dying Lord, I ask but to be Thine;
> My life in Thee, Thy life in me, makes heaven
> forever mine."

Nurses and visitors were huddled outside the doorway to Theo's room, all standing in rapt silence, some on the verge of tears. Jessica placed her guitar back in its case. Taking her father's thin hand in her own—she wept—bitterly.

Pastor Theo Cross found freedom at last, like snow melting on a warm windowpane—melting away peacefully, inevitably, and almost imperceptibly. Pastor Theo Cross slipped from life to death, to life—free from pain, free from life's sorrows, free for a life beyond. Pastor Theo Cross slipped into the Mystery, as shadow fades to dawn.

Weeks later Doris attended to her husband's grave. Their plot was located at the far end of the cemetery, near a stone wall, nestled in the shade of an ancient oak tree. In her hand she held bright yellow daffodils she'd gathered from their garden. Placing them on the grave, she read the words etched on the stone: "As long as a man breathes he should not lose hope!" The limbs of the old oak were already beginning to breathe hope of new life come spring: a whisper of springtime, even as the grip of winter began to relent and release its hold. Doris knelt down, bowed her head in devotional silence. She thought about life and death, about Theo and his ministry, about their love and devotion and years of dedicated passion—about God—and the truth of God's *amazing grace*.

The End

Epilogue

LONG AFTER THE DEATH of Theo Cross, his family and friends discovered that his life, as a story of God's amazing grace, continued to live within their own stories—giving evidence to the impact this one human life had made in conferring grace upon the hearts and souls of those touched by all that was Theo Cross. So often we fail to see or hear the personal story of another, someone immediate to and intimate with us, someone we love and are loved by in return, because their story is still being written, and perhaps even edited. But once that soul is no longer with us, his or her story is somehow integrated into the narrative of our own identity; thereafter, we no longer define ourselves without reference to that other narrative, the story of our lost friend, family member, spouse, or lover. It is then that we awaken to the way in which our stories are woven into a larger tapestry of human existence—not unlike the poetic observation that no one is an "island" unto self alone.

Human life is one seamless fabric of grace, as God intends for us to intertwine and find personal fulfillment and enrichment in our participation in the life of another—in the collective lives of those around us. My story has no reference point if it has not been influenced, shaped, and transformed by the stories of those others who have joined me in this journey called "life." God's grace, following the profound event of the Incarnation of His Son, is most evident in the interdependency of the narratives unfolding both within and around us. The deepest meaning of life—human life—is located in the way the personal stories of others influence the person we are, are becoming, and will become; and the way in which our story then gives testimony to the transforming effect the stories of others have on our own sense of self. God's grace is always incarnational; faith is always experienced within the context of relationships. Personal stories are more than an account of someone's earthly existence, rather they are woven narratives of that which has given meaning and purpose to that individual's life, disclosing the essential life experiences that have formed his or her personal identity: an identity which is a composite narrative, also and always indebted to those with whom one has lived and moved and been transformed in this world.

Even the life of a fictional character, like Theo Cross, is graced by the lives of others. In the end, we measure the impact of any one human life in terms of the way in which his or her narrative has been shaped by, and helped shape, the personal stories of family, friends, lovers—and yes—even strangers.